NO TURNING BACK . . .

Out of nowhere a rash voice inside her head whispered: *Why not try the brush fence? Just see how he takes it. Then you'll really know what you're dealing with.* Lisa's hands began to sweat. Reason told her to wait. But just this once she didn't feel like listening to reason. She eyed the brush from twenty yards away. It was at least two feet higher than the tires, and with the shrubbery reaching up from its wooden box it looked even higher. Lisa told herself she was going to think about it. But riding Samson in a circle, she realized she was only lining up to get a better approach. She knew she was going to take the fence. Her confidence was up; there was no turning back.

THE SADDLE CLUB

SECRET
HORSE

BONNIE BRYANT

A SKYLARK BOOK
NEW YORK · TORONTO · LONDON · SYDNEY · AUCKLAND

RL 5, 009–012

SECRET HORSE

A Bantam Skylark Book / March 1999

ISBN 0-553-48671-3

Published simultaneously in the United States and Canada.

Bantam Books are published by Bantam Books, a division of Random House, Inc. Its
trademark, consisting of the words "Bantam Books" and the portrayal of a rooster, is
Registered in U.S. Patent and Trademark Office and in other countries. Marca
Registrada. Bantam Books, 1540 Broadway, New York, New York 10036.

PRINTED IN THE UNITED STATES OF AMERICA

OPM   0 9 8 7 6 5 4 3 2 1

*I would like to express my special thanks
to Caitlin Macy for her
help in the writing of this book.*

CAROLE HANSON BREATHED deeply. There was no better combination of smells than freshly mown grass and horses. And, she reflected, standing outside Pine Hollow Stables, there was no better time than the early morning in summer. For as long as she could remember, summer vacation had meant one thing: more time to spend at the barn. What made summers even nicer was that Carole shared them with her two best friends, Stevie Lake and Lisa Atwood. Stevie and Lisa were almost as horse-crazy as she was. They would be arriving soon. But for now, except for the stable employees, she had Pine Hollow to herself.

Carole paused before going in to greet her horse. The scene was arresting. A small group of young horses frolicked in the pasture that stretched out before her.

There were two chestnuts, a bay, a gray, and one pure black. Carole smiled as the black horse bucked and took off down the fence. Whenever she watched this particular young horse, her heart swelled with pride. His name was Samson, and he had been born and bred, and now was being trained, on Pine Hollow grounds. The stable's owner, Max Regnery, had high hopes for Samson, as Carole knew. She lingered a moment longer to watch the young gelding at play. Samson was what horsepeople called a good mover. His gaits were long and even and smooth. He had excellent conformation and a good disposition. That was no surprise, Carole thought. It was just what you'd expect from the son of Cobalt, a fiery black stallion, and Delilah, a gentle palomino mare. Samson seemed to combine the best of his parents' traits.

"Nice picture, huh?" said a low voice beside Carole.

Startled out of her reverie, Carole turned to see the head stable hand, Red O'Malley, standing next to her.

"I'll say," she agreed. "I was just thinking how great Samson looks."

Red nodded. "He's been going great, too," he said. "I only wish Max and I had more time to work with him. We've been so busy, and now . . ."

As Red's voice trailed off, Carole noticed that he was carrying his saddle and had a large duffel bag slung over his back. "Are you going away?" she asked.

2

Red nodded, his eyes bright with anticipation. "Yeah, I got a working student position with Toby MacIntosh. I'm going up to Vermont for a month."

"Wow!" Carole exclaimed. "Congratulations." Toby MacIntosh was a top three-day eventer. He took on working students at his farm every summer and, Carole knew, the positions were extremely hard to get.

"Thanks," Red said modestly. "I just found out yesterday. I was on the waiting list and someone dropped out at the last minute. Max was great about letting me go on such short notice," the stable hand added, a note of worry creeping into his voice.

Carole could read Red's thoughts instantly. "Don't you worry about Max," she said firmly. "Stevie and Lisa and I are planning to hang out here every day. We'll pitch in—muck stalls, clean tack, anything."

"I was hoping you'd say that," Red confessed. His face brightened. "There are horses to be exercised, too, you know, so it won't be all drudgery."

"Even better," Carole said. They both looked out at the pasture again. The horses had settled down and were grazing quietly. "Samson, too?" Carole inquired.

Red nodded vigorously. "Definitely. The more he gets out, the better. In fact, it'll be great to see what the three of you can do with him." As an afterthought, he added, "Drop me a line and let me know how his training is going."

Carole promised to do so. She walked with Red to his pickup truck. "Have fun!" she called as Red started the engine. "And don't work too hard!"

Red gave a jaunty wave and disappeared up the driveway.

Walking into the barn, Carole glanced once more toward the pasture. She couldn't wait to try Samson again. But her own horse came first. And if Carole had learned anything recently, it was that she was happy to keep it that way.

"Starlight!" she called. "Hello, boy!"

The bay gelding stuck his nose out over the stall, nickering faintly. Carole saw that he was chewing on a mouthful of hay. "Okay," she said, laughing, "you finish breakfast and I'll get my grooming kit."

On her way into the tack room, Carole glanced idly at the bulletin board hanging on the wall outside. Max used the board to post notices about horses for sale, stable jobs, boarding fees, and horse shows. Carole had looked at it the day before—and the day before that—and didn't really expect to see anything new. But then she did a double take. Tacked to the cork was a horse show program, and not just any program, but one for the Macrae Valley Open in Pennsylvania.

Carole could feel her heart start to beat a little faster. The Macrae Valley Open was one of the premier horse shows on the East Coast. Carole had dreamed about rid-

4

ing in it since she was a little girl. She had been a spectator on several occasions, and each time she went, her
desire to show there herself had gotten stronger. Besides
being A-rated and having the reputation of attracting
the best riders, the Macrae was particularly famous for its
junior divisions. Many of the best Olympic riders had
cut their teeth riding in the junior jumper division of the
Macrae.

Gingerly, as if she were handling a sacred object, Carole removed the program from the bulletin board. She
flipped through the heavy cream-colored pages with
longing. But when she came to the junior section, she
closed the program abruptly. It was just too hard to read
about a show she couldn't enter. The Macrae was hundreds of miles away. Carole didn't own a horse trailer.
Max, with his busy schedule of coaching, training, and
farm management, could hardly be persuaded to take
one rider that great a distance. Carole wouldn't even
want to ask him. Besides, if Max ever thought she deserved to go, he would mention it himself. That, Carole
thought grimly, tacking the program back to the board,
settled that.

Still, when Lisa and Stevie turned up half an hour
later, Carole couldn't help mentioning the show.

"The Macky Ray—what?" said Stevie, yanking on her
cowboy boots.

"The Macrae Valley Open!" Lisa said. The three girls

5

were changing in the locker room. "Even I've heard of it."

"Well, why don't you just ask Max if you can go?" Stevie suggested. "I'm sure you and Starlight are good enough."

Shaking her head wistfully, Carole explained that it was more complicated than that. She would need transportation, a driver . . .

"Maybe Red could drive you in the Pine Hollow van," Lisa suggested. "I bet he'd love to go to the Macrae. Maybe he could compete as well."

"Oh, I meant to tell you," said Carole. "I just saw Red on his way out. He's going away for a month—to be a working student on Toby MacIntosh's farm. Maybe I'll talk to him about the show when he comes back. But until then, I told him we'd pitch in and make up for his absence."

Stevie groaned good-naturedly. Unlike Carole, who thought mucking stalls was sheer joy, Stevie preferred her days heavy on the riding and light on the barn chores. Still, when the time came to help out, she always did more than her fair share. That was one of the rules of The Saddle Club, a group that she, Lisa, and Carole had started. Members had to be (a) horse-crazy and (b) willing to help each other out in any situation. Because Pine Hollow Stables was the club's unofficial home base, the helping out often took place there.

To soften the blow, Carole added, "Red did say there are horses to be exercised while he's gone, too. Including Samson."

The mention of Samson set the girls talking excitedly. Samson had been a Saddle Club project since day one. Since before day one, actually: since the girls had helped care for his mother, Delilah, while she was in foal. They had also been there at the colt's birth. A local horse trainer, Mr. Grover, had helped Samson through his initial months under saddle, but The Saddle Club had been waiting for him on his return. More recently, they had watched him develop into a real riding horse.

"I saw Red riding him the other day," Lisa remarked. "Samson looked great! He's a really good mover."

"I was just thinking that this morning," Carole said enthusiastically.

Lisa flushed. It made her happy when Carole, the most experienced rider of the three of them, agreed with her opinions.

"Ready, girls?" said Stevie with a grin.

"Ready," Lisa said.

"Let's head 'em up and move 'em out."

Dressed to ride, the girls hurried down the aisle to tack up. All three of them stiffened when they saw who was walking toward them.

"Veronica," Stevie muttered under her breath.

"Well, hello!" cried the new arrival in a singsongy

voice. Veronica diAngelo was also dressed to ride. But unlike The Saddle Club, who wore an assortment of old jeans, T-shirts, and boots, she was wearing brand-new breeches and a show-quality sleeveless riding shirt. "Has anyone seen the program for the Macrae Valley Open?" she inquired loudly.

"You're staring right at it," Stevie said coldly, with an inkling of what Veronica was up to.

"Oh, you're right! Silly me. Here it is, tacked up on the bulletin board." Annoyed, The Saddle Club watched the girl remove the booklet and flip through the pages. "Phew!" Veronica said, pretending to be relieved. "The junior jumper division is scheduled during a weekend. I was afraid it would interfere with my private—"

"Manicures?" Stevie interrupted sweetly. "I'm sure you'll be able to fit them in."

Veronica gave Stevie a pitying look. "Poor Stephanie," she said. "Always trying to get at me, aren't you? I guess that's what the little people do. In their small, pathetic ways, they—"

"Are you going to the Macrae?" Carole broke in.

"Excuse me?" said Veronica.

Carole swallowed as Stevie glared at her. "Are you going to ride in the Macrae?" she repeated. She knew she was playing right into Veronica's scheme by giving

8

her the attention she wanted. But Carole didn't care. She had to know.

"Why, yes, Carole, I am," said Veronica, beaming. "And I expect to do very well. After all, we know how Danny got his name, don't we?"

The Saddle Club rolled their eyes at one another. Danny was only the barn name of Veronica's horse. His real name was Go for Blue—as in "go for blue ribbons." He had been a champion jumper when Veronica bought him, with many trophies to his record.

"Yes, we do know how Danny got his name," Stevie sneered. "Being ridden by people other than you!"

"Stevie Lake!" Veronica sputtered, her face turning red.

"Maybe you should change his name to Go for Pink," Stevie suggested gleefully. Pink was the color of the fifth-place ribbon.

"Stevie . . . ," Lisa said warningly. She knew from experience that Stevie and Veronica's little tiffs could quickly escalate into major feuds.

Veronica snapped the program shut. "I knew I shouldn't have mentioned the Macrae!" she cried. "I knew you'd all just be . . . jealous! It's not my fault that none of you has horses that are good enough for top competition!" Veronica paused, glancing hastily at Carole.

9

The Saddle Club said nothing—not Carole, not Lisa, not even Stevie. But they all knew what the sidelong glance meant: In her heart of hearts, Veronica knew Starlight was as good as Danny—maybe better. Carole's father hadn't paid a lot of money for Starlight, and Carole had trained the horse herself without fancy private instructors. But Carole had trained him well, and over fences, the two of them were the team to beat.

After momentarily holding her tongue, Stevie couldn't resist getting in another little dig. "I wonder if Danny will even be up to his old level," she mused aloud.

"What do you mean, 'his old level'?" snapped Veronica.

Stevie pretended to be surprised. "Well, you know—the level he was at when you bought him. I mean, since you've owned Danny, he hasn't really brought home tons of blues, has he? At least, not that I can remember . . ."

Stevie had turned away, prepared to ignore Veronica's cries of outrage, when she happened to catch sight of Max Regnery walking toward them. In a flash she had pasted a smile on her face and was elbowing Veronica to be quiet.

"Huh?" said Veronica, a fraction of a second before she and Stevie, in a rare moment of unity, called, "Hello, Max!"

"HELLO," SAID MAX dryly, showing he hadn't been fooled by the cover-up. "Are you ready for your lesson, Veronica?"

The Saddle Club exchanged glances. Normally they all had a group lesson together. Evidently Veronica was paying to take private lessons as well.

"*I'm* ready, yes," said Veronica. "So if Red has Danny tacked up . . ."

"Red had to leave early this morning. You'll have to tack Danny up yourself today," Max replied tersely.

Stevie snickered, but Veronica had an immediate comeback.

"All right," she said. "But thank goodness Daddy hired me my own private show groom for the Macrae!"

With that, she pinned the program back to the bulletin board and disappeared into the tack room.

The Saddle Club all looked at Max. Max looked back. "Yes?" he asked. "Is there something you need?"

Carole couldn't speak. Lisa didn't know what to say. So Stevie jumped right in. "So, Max, I was just thinking . . ."

"I'll bet you were," Max murmured.

" . . . if Veronica's going to the Macrae, you must be taking the big Pine Hollow van. And that means you have four stalls to fill . . ."

Noticing the skeptical look on Max's face, Lisa suddenly had an idea. Stevie was going about this all wrong! "Er, Max?" she interrupted, giving Stevie a significant look.

"Yes, Lisa?"

"I think what Stevie meant to ask you is what we can do to help around here while Red's gone."

Max beamed. "Now, that's an excellent question. In my office there's a list of horses to be exercised."

"Great," said Stevie, catching on. "Why don't we go tack up right away?"

"Well"—Max hesitated—"only one horse really needs to go out today." He grinned as he added, "But there's another list on my desk of—"

"Barn chores," Stevie finished for him.

"How did you know?" Max said innocently.

"Wild guess," muttered Stevie.

"Who's the horse?" Carole called hopefully as their instructor started down the aisle.

"Samson," Max called back. "I guess you can draw straws."

"I'VE ALWAYS PREFERRED paper, scissors, rock," Stevie said when Max had gone.

"How does that go again?" Carole asked.

"Scissors cuts paper, paper covers rock, and rock smashes scissors," Lisa chimed in.

"Okay: you and me, Carole," said Stevie. "Two out of three."

Carole beat Stevie. Then she and Lisa played. For some reason Lisa felt nervous. When she won she breathed a sigh of relief.

"I knew I should have stuck with rock!" Carole said. But the truth was, she was just as happy to ride Starlight that afternoon. "I've got an idea," she added. "Why don't Stevie and I get going on Max's list while Lisa exercises Samson, and then in the afternoon we can all ride our own horses, together?"

Stevie grumbled but let herself be persuaded. She and Carole headed off to Max's office.

Lisa grabbed a halter and walked toward the pasture. She whistled on the way. She felt incredibly lucky to be the one to ride Samson. If they hadn't played for it, Lisa

13

knew she would have let Carole or Stevie ride instead. After all, Carole was more experienced than she was. And Stevie was more confident. And both experience and confidence were very important when it came to training a green horse. But given the chance, Lisa knew she could do it.

At the pasture rail she put her fingers to her lips and whistled the way Stevie had taught her. Most of the horses ignored her and went on grazing. But Samson recognized the call. He raised his head and pricked up his ears. When Lisa whistled again, he came to her at a trot. "Hello, boy," Lisa murmured, patting his fine, silky neck. Gently she buckled the halter over his head and snapped a white cotton lead to it. Even at a walk Samson was spectacular. At 16.3 hands, he was a big horse, but his lines were delicate. His dark coat shone in the summer sun. It had been months since any of the girls had ridden him; now Lisa couldn't wait to see what he was like.

IN THE COOL of the barn, Lisa cross-tied Samson close to where her friends were scrubbing out buckets. That way they could all talk. And talking, among The Saddle Club, was a way of life. After greeting Samson, Stevie and Carole got back to the topic of the morning: the Macrae Valley Open. The very thought of it excited Carole.

"Lisa's got the idea. If we work hard, why wouldn't Max let you ride?" Stevie asked, turning on the hose.

Carole frowned. "A lot of reasons. One, Veronica might have rented out the whole van. Two, he might not think I'm ready. Three . . . Three . . ." Carole faltered, scrub brush in hand. "I can't think of a three," she admitted.

"It sounds like you're trying hard to think of reasons why you *can't* go," Stevie remarked.

"Heck, I don't know!" said Carole. "Maybe we can all go! The whole Saddle Club with Prancer, Belle, and Starlight. How does that sound?"

Stevie laughed. "That sounds more like it."

"So what's it like?" Lisa asked curiously, trading her currycomb for a body brush. "The Macrae, I mean. Is it like Briarwood?"

Briarwood was a top-rated horse show in which the girls had competed, with mixed results. Carole contemplated Lisa's question. "Ye-es," she said slowly. "I guess you could say the Macrae is like Briarwood. Only it's . . . bigger. And better. Briarwood gets all the best riders—from here. But the Macrae gets *all* the best riders, period. The last event is always the Grand Prix. The USET members turn out in full force."

"Wow," Lisa breathed. As she and Stevie knew, *USET* stood for "United States Equestrian Team." Riding for "the Team" was every rider's dream. At Pine

15

Hollow, people often said that Carole would make the Team someday—if she stuck with horses. And—Lisa laughed, watching Carole attack the grime on a water bucket—there was little doubt she would stick with horses!

"What's so funny?" Stevie said.

Lisa giggled again. "Just Carole's enthusiasm for scrubbing buckets."

"You're telling me," Stevie groaned. "This is the worst barn chore ever."

"That's what you said last week about raking the driveway," Carole noted wryly.

"This time I mean it!" Stevie insisted. "It's a ton of work and the buckets don't even look that different afterward."

"But think how much the horses appreciate it," Carole pointed out.

Stevie frowned. "Belle and I had a talk and she told me a little grime makes the water taste better."

At Carole's raised eyebrows Stevie hastily added, "But tell us more about the Macky Ray. It'll keep me inspired to scrub."

Carole didn't need to be asked twice. Lost in her fantasy of riding in the show, she described the beautiful grounds, the beautiful horses, the beautiful fences—

"What about the riders?" Stevie joked. "I hope they're beautiful, too."

16

Carole frowned. She thought for a minute. "I guess that depends on whether you mean beautiful outside or beautiful inside."

"Both, of course!" Stevie replied. "Like us!"

Carole smiled, but her voice was serious when she explained that many of the teenagers who rode the A circuit (meaning they competed in top-level shows all year) were not the nicest people she'd ever met.

"But what about Kate Devine?" Lisa said. "She was a champion at those shows."

Kate Devine, the daughter of an old friend of Carole's father, was now an old friend of The Saddle Club's. Kate had ridden the circuit for years, with great success, until she decided that the competitiveness among the riders was spoiling her love of horses. With The Saddle Club's help, Kate had rediscovered her love of riding, but now she was happy living on her family's ranch out West, where the only riding she did was for pleasure.

"Kate's the exception, not the rule," Carole answered. "Because she *is* nice. And modest. And she puts her horse first—not the blue ribbon. And because whatever trophies she took home, you know she worked really hard for. A lot of the girls who compete at shows like the Macrae are pretty spoiled, and they're snobby."

"So what you're saying is that they're all like . . . Veronica?" Stevie suggested.

Carole didn't deny it. "These girls have their own trainers, grooms . . . They pay people to braid their horses' manes and tails, they spend more money than—"

"They *pay* people to braid for them?" cried Lisa. "Gosh, maybe Stevie should go into business."

"I think Lisa may be on to something," Stevie said. "I'd make a killing." While Lisa was expert at any kind of handiwork, such as embroidery and needlepoint, Stevie was The Saddle Club expert at mane and tail braiding. At horse show time, her services were much in demand. "In fact," Stevie continued, "I could drop out of school and take it on the road. I could live out of a suitcase, sleep under the stars . . ."

Carole and Lisa grinned. With Stevie, any conversation could be turned into a plan to drop out of school.

". . . hang out at truck stops, eat in diners— Say," Stevie interrupted herself. "You never told us what the food was like at the Macrae, Carole."

"I was coming to that," Carole said, her dark eyes twinkling. "The food is top quality, too. It's not just hot dogs and hamburgers."

"But they do *have* hot dogs and hamburgers, don't they?" Stevie asked worriedly.

"Oh, yes. But they also have gourmet sandwiches and salads and"—Carole paused dramatically—"a separate stand for ice cream."

18

"Ice cream at the Macrae? We're going!" Stevie declared.

Leaving her friends to discuss the chances of convincing Max, Lisa went to the tack room to get Samson's bridle and saddle—or, rather, Samson's bridle and her saddle. Most saddles fit most horses; the important thing was that they fit the rider. On Samson, Lisa would use the saddle she normally used when she rode Prancer, another Pine Hollow horse. At most she would have to switch the girth, the beltlike piece of equipment that went around the horse's belly to hold the saddle in place. Bridles, on the other hand, had to fit the horse's head. They could be adjusted, but it was easier for each horse to have its own bridle. That way the fit was always right.

Lisa picked up her saddle and a clean saddle pad. Hesitating a moment, she took a bridle down from the rack and headed back to the cross-ties.

Carole and Stevie had taken a bucket break and were fussing over Samson. "Gosh, you're a pretty boy, aren't you?" cooed Carole.

Stevie rubbed the black horse's neck. "Here, we'll help you tack up," she said.

For just a second Lisa felt herself stiffen. She felt possessive about Samson this morning. She would have preferred to tack him up herself. But almost as quickly, she realized how silly she was being. She relaxed and handed Stevie the saddle. "Thanks," she said. "I hope Prancer's girth fits."

"It will," Carole predicted confidently. "They're about the same height, and they have similar conformation. Samson's shoulder slopes a bit more, which will make his gaits smoother, and Prancer is fuller through the barrel, but that's just because . . ."

As Carole prattled on, Lisa looped the reins over Samson's neck and removed his halter. She was only half listening. Sometimes Carole could sound like a know-it-all, even though Lisa knew she was just being enthusiastic.

When Samson took the bit, Lisa slid the headpiece of the bridle over his ears. She buckled the noseband and the throatlatch. She was all set to go.

". . . fit of the bridle is more important anyway because—" Carole paused suddenly. She stepped forward and looked at Samson's head. "Lisa, you've got the wrong bridle. That one doesn't fit. See how the bit is hanging in his mouth? It's much too low."

Frowning, Lisa looked more closely. Carole was right. Lisa felt herself redden.

"I know which one it is. I'll go get it," Carole offered.

When she was gone, Stevie whispered excitedly to Lisa, "Are you thinking what I'm thinking?"

"Um . . . ," Lisa said. Not knowing what Stevie was getting at, she busied herself with taking off the bridle.

"I'm thinking that we've got to figure out a way to get Carole to the Macrae! It would be her dream come true!"

"Yeah," said Lisa, trying to muster enthusiasm, "I guess it would."

Mounted on Samson, Lisa had no trouble being enthusiastic. It was all she could do not to grin from ear to ear. Riding the gelding was a dream in itself. He had a wonderful spring in his step, even at the walk. At the trot he arched his neck and strutted along proudly. It made Lisa proud just to be sitting on his back. His canter was even better. On Prancer, a former racehorse, cantering felt fast. But on Samson it was smooth and rhythmic. Lisa could have cantered all day, it was so pleasant in the outdoor ring with the sun shining and a few old oaks to offer shade. But she didn't want Samson to get bored just going around and around. While she decided what to do next, Lisa slowed to a walk and loosened the reins so that the gelding could stretch his neck.

At the end of the ring were two semipermanent

jumps: a set of tires and a larger brush fence. They were used for schooling. Both fences were typical of the kind of obstacles a rider might encounter in a horse show. Looking at them, Lisa's thoughts wandered back to the Macrae. The truth was, she was just the tiniest bit jealous of Carole. Or not exactly jealous. At the end of the day, Lisa would be happy if Carole got to ride in the show. But she couldn't help wishing *she* could ride in it, too. The way Carole talked about it made it sound like so much fun, and so exciting. "Well," Lisa said aloud, "maybe we'll all get to go, eh, Samson? But more likely, Veronica will go alone."

Putting that thought out of her head, Lisa tightened the reins and asked for a trot. For twenty minutes she worked on dressage. She trotted circles and practiced transitions from walk to trot, trot to canter, and back down. Samson wasn't perfect—no horse was, and he was still green. He got playful and Lisa had to concentrate to control him. But his willingness was a very good sign. He seemed eager to please, despite his high spirits— which, Lisa thought, was exactly what you'd expect from a horse with both excellent breeding and excellent training.

After a final transition from canter to sitting trot, Lisa found herself heading on a line toward the small tire jump. She hardly even thought twice. Jumping logically followed flat work. She shortened her reins, rose slightly in her stirrups, and guided Samson toward the jump. When he got close to it, the black gelding pricked up his ears, stood way back, and took a huge leap. Unprepared, Lisa was thrown forward on his neck. "Whoa!" she cried, scrambling quickly back into the saddle. Then she giggled. Even though it had unseated her, the jump had been fun.

When she had steadied Samson, Lisa turned him around and headed back toward the fence from the other direction. This time she guided him more firmly. With her seat, legs, and hands, Lisa encouraged the young horse to trot down to the base of the fence. He still over-jumped by about two feet, but this time he took off from the right place. Lisa was ecstatic. "Good boy!" she exclaimed, patting him on the neck. "Very good boy!"

Lisa trotted Samson and then cantered him over the jump several times. Samson seemed to love what they were doing. Lisa found herself wishing there were a real course set up. "I wonder how much Red's been jumping you," she said to him.

Then, all at once, something occurred to Lisa: Maybe Red hadn't been jumping Samson at all. Lisa drew her breath in sharply. Was that possible? She certainly hadn't heard Red mention anything about it. Could this be Samson's first time? Could she, Lisa Atwood, have ridden Samson over his first real fence? But he had taken

24

to it so naturally! Lisa thought hard. Samson's sire had been a wonderful jumper. Sadly, Cobalt had died jumping, when his rider had put him into a fence so wrong even he couldn't get out of it. That rider, Lisa recalled grimly, was Veronica diAngelo. But Lisa didn't want to dwell on the past, not just now. A two-part question was forming in her mind. Could Samson have inherited his sire's ability? If so, did anyone know?

Her head whirling with these and more questions, Lisa again shortened the reins. She wanted to try the tire jump one more time. This time she would really pay attention to Samson's form over the fence. Granted, that would be easier to judge from the ground. But you could tell a lot from on top, too. Lisa craned her neck to focus on the two fences. The brush loomed huge, dwarfing the tires beside it. And then, out of nowhere, a rash voice inside her head whispered: *Why not try the brush? Just see how he takes it. Then you'll really know what you're dealing with*. Lisa's hands began to sweat. Reason told her to wait. She should get Carole and Stevie to watch, maybe even let Carole be the one to take him over the bigger fence. . . . But just this once Lisa didn't feel like listening to reason. She eyed the brush from twenty yards away. It was a formidable obstacle. It was at least two feet higher than the tires, and with the shrubbery reaching up from its wooden box it looked even higher. "I'll just think about it," Lisa told herself. But riding

Samson in a circle, she realized she was only lining up to get a better approach. She knew she was going to take the fence. Her confidence was up; there was no turning back.

They cantered down to the jump. Instinctively Lisa let Samson pick up speed. She sat tight in the saddle, looking between Samson's black ears, focusing on a point beyond the brush. All at once the fence loomed ahead. There were four strides—then three, two, one— "Go!" Lisa cried, releasing the reins as she pressed her hands into the black mane. Beneath her Lisa felt Samson's knees snap up—they were in the air! She had a split second of nausea before they landed, wondering how the ground could be so far away, and then they were on the other side, galloping along the rail of the ring.

"Whoo-hoo!" Lisa yelled, Stevie-style, standing up in her stirrups. "We did it! We did it!" She reached down to give Samson a huge pat. "We did it all by ourselves!" she whispered.

Cooling down, Lisa *really* couldn't wipe the grin off her face. She had jumped the big brush! Only the best riders at Pine Hollow practiced over that fence—and she had jumped it! And it had been easy! She hadn't worried for a moment that Samson would run out or refuse the fence, or that she would mess up the approach. She had simply felt excited and confident— more confident than she had ever felt before. Maybe

26

that was what riding a great horse was like: pure fun. She couldn't wait to tell Stevie and Carole. Samson was a great jumper! And she had discovered it!

Lost in her reverie, Lisa happened to glance up toward the barn and see her two friends standing there, looking in her direction. A nervous pang hit her in the stomach. How much had they seen?

"Lunch break!" Stevie called.

"Fifteen minutes!" Carole yelled, cupping her hands to her mouth. "We'll help you untack!"

"Great!" Lisa called, waving. "I'll be up in a minute!"

Lisa jumped off and rolled up her stirrups. Loosening his girth, she checked underneath to see how sweaty Samson was. Because she had spent the past fifteen minutes walking, the horse was cool enough to go back to the barn. But Lisa decided to take another lap around the ring on foot. "Just to be safe," she told herself, glancing toward the stable. She couldn't wait to share her discovery with Stevie and Carole. And yet . . . somehow she could. Right now the brush was her and Samson's secret. And for whatever reason, a part of her liked it that way.

"Hurry it up, Lisa!"

Lisa looked up to see Stevie and Carole again. Only now they were barreling toward the ring.

"We're starving so we came to get you!" Carole announced breathlessly.

"Yeah, we worked up a healthy appetite on the bucket brigade," Stevie said as the two of them ducked through the fence.

"A healthy appetite?" Lisa said. "So I guess that means you're going to eat health food?"

"Not that healthy!" Stevie cried. "I already fed my carrot sticks to Belle. Now if only I could get her to like green salad . . ."

Lost in the joking, Lisa felt her anxiety vanish.

"Good ride?" Carole asked.

"Great ride," said Lisa. "I'll tell you all about it at lunch."

WITH THE THREE of them working, it took no time at all to untack Samson, groom him, and turn him out again. Minutes later The Saddle Club members were swapping sandwich halves at their favorite lunch spot, the knoll overlooking Pine Hollow.

After half a peanut butter sandwich, Lisa brought up the subject on her mind. "Does either of you know if Red or Max has been jumping Samson?" she inquired.

"I think Red has been taking him over obstacles on the trail," Carole said.

"But not in the ring?" asked Lisa.

"Well, the trail is the best place to introduce a horse to jumping," Carole replied.

28

Before Lisa could explain why she was interested, Carole went on. "Horses are natural jumpers. So it's best to let them jump naturally. If they get used to hopping over fallen logs, streams, small ditches, it's easier to move to jumping in the ring. Especially if there are natural-looking obstacles in the ring, such as—"

"The brush in the outdoor ring here?" Lisa interrupted, almost shaking with excitement.

"Well, yes," Carole agreed, "except of course you'd start out with much, much smaller fences."

"Of course," said Lisa, a smile playing on her lips.

"Why?" Carole asked curiously. "Were you thinking of jumping Samson?"

"Now, there's an idea!" Stevie put in. "He ought to be great. He is Cobalt's son, after all."

Carole liked the idea as well. "Maybe tomorrow we can set up some trotting poles and see how he does. Then after a week or two, we can try him over a cross rail, something small that won't worry him, eighteen inches or so. If that works . . ."

Listening to Carole's chatter, Lisa felt her smile grow. She knew what Carole was saying made sense. But she also knew that she and Samson had just jumped the biggest fence on Pine Hollow property! The secret made her happy. It was fun, too, that for once she knew more than Carole.

When Carole finished outlining the training program, Lisa couldn't wait another minute. She had to share her discovery.

"We might be able to take Samson's training a little faster than that," she suggested.

"You mean because of his breeding?" said Carole. "Because that's important, but it's not everything. Right now we have no idea how Samson—"

"Yes, we do," Lisa broke in. "At least I do." At Carole's and Stevie's blank looks, she explained, "I jumped Samson today."

"You did?" said Stevie, putting down her sandwich. "That's great. How'd he do?"

Lisa paused for a second before answering, anticipating her friends' reaction to the news she was about to give. Then she said slowly, looking from Stevie to Carole, "He did amazingly well. Judging by his performance today, I think it's fair to say that Samson is a very, very talented jumper."

"Really? Wow," said Stevie. "What a great discovery."

Lisa looked at Carole to see how she was taking the news. To her surprise, Carole didn't look particularly excited. "Did you set up fences down at the ring?" she asked curiously.

Lisa shook her head. "No, I jumped him over the permanent obstacles, the . . . the tires," she said after a moment's hesitation.

"The tires? Those are a good two feet," Carole said thoughtfully. "Did you jump him more than once?"

"Several times," Lisa said proudly. "Each time he was better than the first."

"It sounds like he really liked it," Carole remarked.

"Why shouldn't he?" Lisa said a touch defensively. "I'm telling you, he's a natural." Excitedly, she began to describe what jumping Samson was like.

"I can't wait to see Samson jump myself," Carole said.

Lisa frowned. Her big news had barely made an impression on Carole. What she ought to do was tell Carole about the brush. That would get her attention for sure. But Lisa stubbornly felt she didn't want to mention it. That jump, at least, she wanted to keep secret.

"Me either," Stevie was saying. "Why don't we take him out in a group tomorrow morning? Same time, same place."

"Perfect," Carole said. "We can take turns riding him."

"Oh, darn!" Lisa cried, remembering. "I won't be able to make it. I'm going to D.C. with my mother tomorrow. I promised her I would go to a museum at least once a month. She wants me to learn to appreciate art."

"What about the fine art of horsemanship?" Stevie said indignantly. "Doesn't that count?"

Lisa sighed. "Not in her book. The closest I'll get to horsemanship tomorrow is a painting of a horse."

31

"Come late," Carole urged. "We'll wait until the afternoon to ride Samson."

"That's okay," said Lisa. "You guys go ahead and I'll help out with mucking stalls in the afternoon."

When Carole and Stevie protested, Lisa insisted. It was only fair that they get a turn after scrubbing buckets all morning. But that was only part of it. The truth was, she was almost relieved she wasn't going to be there when her friends rode Samson. Even the idea of it made her the slightest bit jealous. Carole, especially, had been very possessive of Samson in the past, partly due to her love for Cobalt. When Samson had gone to live at Mr. Grover's for a time, Carole had seemed to get over this possessiveness. But, Lisa thought, chewing anxiously on a fingernail, it could always come back . . .

4

THE NEXT MORNING Carole's and Stevie's muscles were aching from the extra-long day they had put in. By the time they had ridden their own horses and helped with the evening chores, it had been nearly dark. Now they were back two hours after sunrise. But they wouldn't have had it any other way. They loved getting into the groove of the stable, being there for the morning feeding and the evening haying. This morning, as they went from stall to stall filling water buckets, each was lost in her own thoughts.

Carole kept going over what Lisa had said. She hadn't stopped thinking about it all night. But though she desperately wanted to believe in Samson's talent, sight unseen, inwardly she forced herself to be skeptical. She knew from experience that a horse's talent—for any-

33

thing—could not be judged instantaneously. While there was no doubt that Lisa had enjoyed jumping Samson, her enthusiasm might have run away with her.

But there was another reason Carole had to see the horse jump for herself. Ever since Cobalt had died, Carole had hoped Samson would inherit his sire's talent. If what Lisa said was true, then Cobalt's legacy would truly live on. But Carole didn't want to get her hopes up only to be disappointed.

Stevie, meanwhile, was picturing herself moving out West with Belle. The two of them could live out on the range, sleep under the stars. She'd have a guitar strapped to her back. She'd play old favorites around the campfire—like "Git Along, Little Dogies" and "I've Been Working on the Railroad" and—

"Uh, Stevie?"

"Yeah?"

"Any particular reason why you just launched into 'Home on the Range'?"

Stevie grinned. "Just thinking about the future," she said.

Carole laughed. The girls knew each other so well, Stevie didn't have to explain any more than that.

They also knew that whenever one of them was absent, the other two felt it. Tacking up Samson, Stevie said she wished Lisa didn't have to be at the museum.

"Especially since she's the one who made the discovery about how great a jumper Samson is."

Carole hesitated. Then she said, her voice dry, "Stevie, let's wait and see before we draw any conclusions about Samson's ability."

"Sure," Stevie said, "but Lisa sounded pretty certain."

"I hope she's right," Carole said quietly.

Stevie gave her a sharp look. All at once she understood. It wasn't that Carole doubted Lisa, it was that she was afraid to trust her. That was very different.

When Samson was bridled and saddled, the two girls walked him down to the outside ring. "Why don't you ride him?" Carole said hoarsely.

Stevie nodded, noticing how shaky Carole sounded. "Sounds good."

Carole gave her a leg up and then dropped back to watch horse and rider warm up. Again she noticed what a nice mover Samson was. After twenty minutes or so, Stevie shortened her stirrups a couple of holes and prepared to jump. Carole set up two low cross rails a few strides apart. Perched on the rail of the ring, she was almost afraid to look as Stevie trotted Samson toward the first. But as soon as she saw one jump, Carole couldn't take her eyes off them.

Samson was spectacular. Like most green horses, he over-jumped, clearing every fence by a two-foot margin.

But in the air his form was picture-perfect. He rounded his back and snapped up his knees. In spite of herself, Carole laughed delightedly. "He looks like he's trying to convince us to raise the fences!" she called to Stevie, "and give him something real to jump!"

"He's got such a big jump I can hardly stay in the saddle!" Stevie hollered.

Eventually, tiring of the cross rails, Stevie rode Samson over the tires as Lisa had done. Watching the black horse soar over the fence, Carole couldn't hold in her enthusiasm. She sprang from the rail, clapping her hands together. "Yippee!" she cried, jumping up and down and hugging herself. Her relief and excitement were enormous. What she had hardly permitted herself to think about was now a reality. Eyes shining, Carole found herself whispering over and over again, "He's going to be good, Cobalt! He's going to be just like you!"

BEFORE CALLING IT a day, Carole tried Samson herself. She didn't want to overdo it, so she jumped him over only a few fences. But it was enough—enough to confirm that Lisa was dead right. Carole had jumped dozens of horses in the years she'd been riding. Very few—only a handful—made her feel the way Samson did. It was an edge they had over other horses. An Olympic horse she'd once ridden had had it. Cobalt had had it. It was the feeling, simply, that the horse could jump anything that

36

was set before him. Her heart pounding with happiness, Carole vaulted lightly off Samson's back.

Seeing the expression on Carole's face, Stevie didn't have to ask her friend what she thought. She knew that in the past hour, one of Carole's dreams had come true.

"YOU KNOW," CAROLE said, walking back to the barn, "Samson would make a great junior jumper. He'd make a great jumper, period, but why should the adults have all the fun? Max doesn't need another show horse."

"Whereas *we* . . . ," Stevie continued, hazel eyes twinkling.

". . . definitely need another Saddle Club project!" Carole finished for her.

They walked a few paces in silence, then Stevie stopped dead in her tracks. She grasped Carole's arm. "Carole," she said in a low, urgent voice, "we also need a way to convince Max to take us to the Macrae."

Carole stared at her. "Are you suggesting . . . ?" Stevie nodded. The idea was wild. It was impossible. It was—"Fantastic," Carole breathed.

"Do you think we could get him ready in time?" Stevie murmured, hardly daring to consider the reality of what she was saying.

Carole surveyed the horse beside her. Her mind seemed to be spinning yet focused at the same time. "It's hard to say," she said slowly. "He's talented, but he's green. And it's a big show. A *very* big show. But we wouldn't have to tell anyone what we were doing."

Stevie waited, wanting to shriek with enthusiasm at the very idea.

Carole was still being practical. "We'd teach Samson a lot just by trying," she said reflectively. She gave the horse's black neck a pat. "It could be our secret, couldn't it, boy?"

"And if it didn't work out, only The Saddle Club would know," said Stevie.

"But if it did work out . . ." Carole allowed herself a shiver of excitement. "Imagine Max's face when he sees us give a jumping demonstration on a horse born and bred right here at Pine Hollow!"

But Stevie's mind had already raced far, far ahead. Her eyes narrowed. "Imagine Veronica diAngelo's face," she said, "when our secret horse jumps the pants—or the saddle—off Danny at the Macrae Valley Open!" In anticipation of that marvelous day, Stevie threw her arms around Samson's neck. "If you beat Veronica," she promised, "you can have my lunch-box carrots for a whole year!"

Talking a mile a minute, the two girls began to make plans for putting Project Secret Horse into action. They couldn't wait to fill Lisa in on the scheme her discovery had hatched.

* * *

LISA HUNG BACK from the crowd, her stomach growling. She had long ago lost track of the number of galleries she had walked through. Mrs. Atwood, of course, had insisted that they take the guided tour. Or as Lisa had begun to think of it, the extremely slow, boring tour that kept them from eating lunch.

"So we have the black figure on red, and the red figure on black . . . ," the woman droned on.

Lisa was an intellectual girl. She was interested in art and music. Normally she might have enjoyed a morning learning about Greek vases. But this morning all she could think of was how fast she could get to Pine Hollow. Making sure no one was looking, she glanced at her watch. Eleven-thirty. By now, Carole and Stevie would have tried Samson. What if they didn't agree with her? What if Carole didn't think Samson was that great a jumper? Yesterday she had acted as if she doubted Lisa's judgment. Lisa bristled at the memory. Maybe Carole had been riding the longest, but Lisa knew a lot about horses, too. Carole could at least trust her opinion!

"Isn't this fascinating?" Mrs. Atwood whispered. The group followed the tour guide into the next room.

Lisa looked up and saw another twenty or thirty groups of Greek vases. "Utterly, Mom. Utterly fascinating," she repeated in a monotone as her thoughts raced back to Pine Hollow.

A second fear struck Lisa. What if Carole and Stevie

did agree with her assessment? Then it wouldn't matter that she had made the discovery. They would have just as much stake in riding Samson as she had. For some reason, this bothered Lisa. She almost wished she hadn't said anything. Maybe she could have trained Samson on her own . . .

As the guide wrapped up her tour, Lisa fell into a daydream. She was riding Samson over a huge course of jumps. People were cheering for them. It was a big horse show. It was . . . the Macrae Valley Open! Snapping out of her fantasy, Lisa looked around sheepishly. She was embarrassed at even having dreamed about riding Samson in the Macrae. Talk about a far-fetched idea! If anyone got to ride in the Macrae it would be Carole, of course. She had the experience, the competence—

"What do you say about getting a little lunch at the museum café?" Mrs. Atwood inquired.

Lisa looked up, grateful for the change of subject. "That sounds excellent, Mom," she said.

Over iced tea and chicken salad, Lisa relaxed and enjoyed herself.

"I'll bet you liked seeing the horses on those vases, didn't you, honey?" Mrs. Atwood asked.

Lisa took a sip of iced tea. "Um, yeah, the horses were great," she said. The truth was, she had been too lost in her thoughts to notice them. She just hadn't been herself since her ride the day before. What was it about jumping Samson, Lisa wondered, that had thrown her so off kilter?

To SAVE TIME, Lisa changed into jeans and a T-shirt in the car. "I wish you'd wear nice breeches to ride in, dear," Mrs. Atwood said absently as they pulled into the driveway at Pine Hollow. "Look, there goes that nice diAngelo girl. And see how nice she *looks*, too— breeches, boots, gloves . . ."

Lisa's eye followed Veronica as she rode Danny toward the outdoor ring. Walking beside the pair was a tall man whom Lisa didn't recognize. No doubt he was a specially imported trainer, there to give Veronica an expensive private lesson.

Whenever Veronica had a big show coming up, the diAngelos called in a battery of instructors to tune up her performance. They seemed to believe that the more famous names they hired, the better their daughter would do.

"I guess she's prepping for the Macrae," Lisa said.

"The Macrae? You mean the Macrae Valley Open in Pennsylvania?" Mrs. Atwood asked curiously.

Lisa could hardly believe her ears. "You've heard of the Macrae, Mom?" she asked incredulously. Mrs. Atwood was usually completely ignorant about horse shows and anything to do with horses.

"Of course I've heard of the Macrae. It's a very important social event in Pennsylvania. There's a black-tie dinner to which all the famous society women go. Boy, would I love to go to that," Mrs. Atwood added wistfully.

Lisa raised her eyebrows in surprise. For once she understood perfectly how her mother felt. "And I'd love to ride in the show, Mom," she said, echoing her mother's tone.

"Well, maybe if you dressed as nicely as Veronica diAngelo, you'd have a better chance," suggested Mrs. Atwood.

Lisa smiled. She could never hope to explain the real situation to her mother—that the reasons Veronica was going to the Macrae were a lot more complicated than wearing good breeches. "Maybe you're right, Mom," she said, not wanting to get into an argument, "but we're not even riding this afternoon. We're mucking stalls. And I wouldn't want to do that in nice breeches."

"You came over here just to muck out stalls?" said Mrs. Atwood, aghast.

Lisa giggled. "Yup."

"Now, that," said Mrs. Atwood, shaking her head, "I will never understand."

"Most people don't, Mom," Lisa said. She got out of the car. "But thanks for the ride."

BEFORE LISA HAD closed the car door, she heard Stevie and Carole chattering excitedly. Carole ran up to greet her with Stevie in tow. "Lisa, you were right! Samson is—"

"In excellent health!" Stevie interrupted. She looked pointedly in the direction of the outdoor ring. Veronica and her instructor were halfway between the ring and the driveway. "Might as well not broadcast the news," Stevie whispered. "There's no telling what she can hear!"

"Whoops!" Carole clapped a hand to her mouth.

At Lisa's confused look, Stevie thought fast and said, "Come on: Saddle Club meeting. Right now. In the hayloft."

"The hayloft?" said Lisa. "Wouldn't the knoll—"

43

"No," said Stevie. "We need total privacy."

Wordlessly the three girls trooped into the barn and climbed the ladder to the loft. They walked to the back and took seats on bales of timothy and alfalfa.

Carole began. Lisa noticed her somewhat formal tone. "Lisa," she explained, "as I started to say outside, you were one hundred percent right about Samson. I think he has the makings of a great jumper."

"You do?" Lisa said excitedly, her worries forgotten.

Carole nodded. A little shyly she added, "The reason I was afraid to believe you before was that—well, I've just been hoping for so long that this would be the case." Carole stopped, choking on her words. She took a deep breath. "Seeing Samson jump was like seeing Cobalt again," she said.

Lisa put out a hand to comfort Carole. Now she understood why Carole had been so cautious the previous day. Cobalt had died a long time before, but Carole still missed the beautiful black stallion. "You had to see Samson jump for yourself before you could believe he had Cobalt's talent, didn't you?" Lisa said.

Carole nodded. Lisa felt a rush of remorse for having taken Carole's reaction personally. But Stevie wouldn't let either of them wallow in apologies. "The point is," she said briskly, "Samson can jump. He's an amazing jumper."

44

"Right," said Carole. "And thanks to you, Lisa, we know that."

"So do you think we should work on training him?" Lisa asked cautiously.

Carole's and Stevie's eyes grew bright. "And how," Stevie said.

"Lisa, we not only want to train Samson," Carole said seriously, "we want to train him for the junior jumper division at the Macrae Valley Open."

"The Macrae—" Lisa started, her daydream coming back to her in a rush.

"We want Samson to be the ace up our sleeve that convinces Max to let us go."

"And our secret weapon against Veronica!" Stevie added.

Lisa leaned back against her stack of hay bales. A range of emotions flooded over her: excitement, fear, envy, hope. She had missed one morning at Pine Hollow, and already her discovery about Samson had taken on a life of its own. "That's great," she managed to say, twisting a handful of hay in her hands. "That's a great idea."

Luckily, Carole and Stevie didn't seem to notice Lisa's conflicting feelings. They chattered on about the training program. They wanted Lisa to map out schedules for them for the next several weeks. "We have to keep up our end with the barn work, that's for sure," Carole pointed out, "or we can kiss our chances at the Macrae good-bye."

Lisa's eyes flew up at the words "our chances." Did that mean Carole thought they were all going to go? "So you mean—" she began, but stopped. Normally Lisa could ask Stevie and Carole anything. That was what best friends were for: answering embarrassing or intimidating questions. But for some reason she couldn't ask them about the Macrae. She couldn't ask them the question that the past twenty-four hours seemed to have been leading up to: If Samson went to the Macrae, which of them would ride him?

AFTER MORE discussion the meeting broke up. The three girls headed back down the ladder to ground level. Veronica had come in from her lesson and was hosing a sweaty Danny off in the wash stall. When she saw The Saddle Club, she beamed smugly. "Hello, girls."

"Hello," the three of them said flatly.

"I'm sorry I didn't see you earlier or I would have introduced you to Tom Riley. He was training me today, and he just left. He sure made us work up a sweat, didn't he, Danny? All those big fences—"

"Who's Tom Riley?" Stevie asked.

"Tom Riley?" Veronica scoffed. "You've never heard of Tom Riley? He's only the best jumper rider under

46

thirty. Haven't you seen his picture plastered on the cover of every riding magazine in the past two years?"

Stevie pretended to think hard. She knew exactly who Tom Riley was. She just didn't want to give Veronica the satisfaction of bragging about her instructor. "Maybe. I really don't remember. Is he a friend of yours?"

"A friend?" said Veronica. "Don't be silly. He was here to give me a lesson. He's one of the people getting me ready for the Macrae."

"Oh, I see," Stevie replied. "So you're *paying* him a lot of *money* to come out here."

"He wouldn't have agreed to teach me if he didn't think I had a lot of potential!" Veronica retorted.

"Really?" said Stevie. "Because now that I think of it, I did read an article about him in *Sporting Horseman*. He said it was really hard to make ends meet as a rider, even when you're as successful as he is. He said he relies on teaching—anyone, anywhere—to pay the bills."

Stifling giggles, Carole and Lisa waited for Veronica to explode. But she clamped her mouth shut, spun around, turned the hose back on, and began to whistle loudly. Stevie's responses often produced that effect. Sometimes Stevie was so quick on the draw that she floored her opponents before they had a chance to open their mouths. And sometimes even Veronica knew to quit when she was ahead—or at least before she was too far behind.

When The Saddle Club had reassembled in the grain room, Lisa let out the laughter she'd been holding in. "Did Tom Riley really say that in *Sporting Horseman*?"

"Nah," Stevie admitted. "I don't even know if he was in *Sporting Horseman*."

Carole frowned. She personally read every equine periodical there was and subscribed to half a dozen. "I've never even *heard* of *Sporting Horseman*," she said, puzzled.

"Me either," Lisa said.

"You haven't heard of *Sporting Horseman*?" Stevie said in a shocked tone, imitating Veronica.

"Uh-uh," said Lisa and Carole.

Stevie grinned. "That's because I made it up."

Carole stared. Lisa shook her head in wonderment. Stevie's talent for winning arguments was awesome.

"Hey, if there's anything I've learned about lying, it's if you're going to lie, lie *big*," Stevie pronounced.

STILL LAUGHING OVER the encounter, the girls kept up the banter as they attacked the stalls that needed cleaning. Stevie dumped the wheelbarrow, and Carole and Lisa filled it. On one of her trips to the manure pile, Stevie was gone longer than usual. "Where were you?" Carole asked. "We've got three loads ready."

48

"Just making sure credit is given where credit is due," Stevie said cryptically.

"Huh?" said Lisa.

Leaning on a pitchfork, Stevie explained that when she had gone to dump the last load, she'd seen Max in the driveway, talking to Mrs. diAngelo. "Normally I wouldn't pass that part of the driveway, but I took the long way around so Max would see me—"

"—and look at your dirty, sweaty face and compare it with Veronica's cool, clean one," Lisa guessed. "Good thinking."

"Thanks," said Stevie. "I also tried to eavesdrop."

"Did you hear anything?" Carole inquired.

"Four words," Stevie said glumly. " 'Van,' 'Macrae,' and 'pay you.' "

Lisa and Carole grimaced. "Somehow I have the feeling a lot of Mrs. diAngelo's conversations end with the words 'pay you,' " Carole said with a sigh. Most of the time she didn't think about how overprivileged Veronica was. But the Macrae bee had gotten into her bonnet. She wanted to go more than anything. And there were times—like when Veronica rented out an entire horse van—that Carole wished, just for once, that she were the spoiled brat instead of the hardworking horsewoman.

Seeing the look on their friend's face, Lisa and Stevie rushed to cheer her up. "Come on, Carole, two more stalls and we're out of here!" Lisa urged.

"With major points from Max!" Stevie said.

Carole smiled. She took up her pitchfork. Thanks to her friends, her moment of envy passed just as quickly as it had come.

THAT EVENING CAROLE sat up in bed, her eyes nearly closed. Her face felt tired from all the sun and fresh air. Her alarm clock was set for 6:45. But before she dropped off to sleep, she wanted to finish her letter to Red. She had started it that morning at breakfast, which now seemed like weeks ago. Carole laughed. So far the card read, "Dear Red"—that was as far as she had gotten. After thinking for a minute, Carole seized her pen and started scrawling.

You wanted me to drop you a line about Samson's progress. Well, would you believe we've decided to turn him into a junior jumper? Lisa tried him over a few fences and discovered his incredible talent. Even with the little I've seen, I really think he could turn out to be as good as Cobalt.

Here Carole paused and chewed on the end of her pen. Then she scribbled out the last sentence. She didn't dare compare Samson to Cobalt—not in writing anyway. She didn't want to jinx the idea! She continued:

We're going to train him like crazy while you're gone. We also had a crazy idea. We want to try to convince Max to let us ride him in the Macrae. If you could only see Samson jump, I think you'd agree we might be able to get him ready.

Carole had nearly come to the end of the page. She was much too tired to contemplate getting out of bed, going downstairs to her father's study, and finding another piece of stationery. "I'd better wrap it up," she decided, wishing she had Lisa's talent for words.

I hope you're having fun up at Toby MacIntosh's. If you have any free time, please write and let me know what you think of our plan.

> Sincerely yours,
> Carole

P.S. The Macrae idea is a SECRET—from Max, Mrs. Reg, everyone, so if you talk to any of them, don't say a word!

Carole really hoped Red would write back and give her some advice. For some reason she felt as if Samson's training rested on her shoulders. Stevie and Lisa would be a huge help, but they would defer to her. If they somehow messed up, if anything happened to Samson, it would be her fault. She would have to explain to Max. She felt slightly sick. She had called the idea crazy in her letter to Red. Was it stupid and reckless as well?

SIX-FORTY-FIVE came before Carole could have believed it possible. Her only comfort came in knowing that two other alarms were going off in Willow Creek. Lisa would be hopping out of bed, too. Stevie, Carole thought with a chuckle, would probably hit the Snooze button a couple of times.

Carole washed and dressed in a fog. She gulped down some orange juice and grabbed a bagel on her way out the door. Carole was lucky in that her father had to be up early and could drive her to Pine Hollow even at this time of day. But in Carole's opinion, Stevie and Lisa were even luckier. They lived close enough to the barn to walk there. It often happened that Carole would meet one of them on the drive over. This morning, spotting a sleepy form trudging along, Colonel Hanson called, "Hop in, Stevie, and save your energy!"

Stevie was glad to obey, even though she had only a hundred yards to go. "Are we really going to do this every day?" she asked Carole. "I might have to start drinking coffee! I haven't felt like this much of a zombie since Halloween!"

Colonel Hanson chuckled and traded bad zombie jokes with Stevie.

As she listened absently, Carole made her mouth form a smile, but her eyes stayed serious. Stevie could guess why. The Saddle Club was about to embark on an incredibly ambitious project. A thousand and one things could go wrong. To comfort her friend, Stevie said, "We'll get him tacked up and out there in no time, huh, Carole?"

Carole let out the breath she'd been holding. "You bet," she said. Focusing on the matter at hand enabled her to relax a little. "We'll take it one day at a time." She gave her father a hug good-bye and followed Stevie into the barn.

As it turned out, they didn't even have to tack up Samson. Lisa had beaten them to it. She was easing the horse's bridle on as Carole and Stevie walked in.

"Wow, you *really* got here early," said Stevie, impressed.

Lisa murmured something about setting her alarm for 5:45 by accident. "I got the right bridle this time. See, Carole?"

Carole nodded. "Yup. Looks good. So far I think we can keep him in the snaffle for jumping," she said, referring to the mild type of bit Samson wore.

"I agree," Lisa said. She wanted to make sure she had just as big a say in the decisions as anyone. She knew as well as Carole that there were many different kinds of bit—the mouthpiece of a bridle—for the many different kinds of horses. Some bits were jointed in the middle, some were straight bars, some had a copper or rubber coating. But any bit was only as good as the hands that held it. A rider with "heavy" hands could ruin a horse's mouth by pulling too roughly or leaning on the reins for balance. Then a horse could get a tough mouth and need a stronger bit. Samson had a nice soft mouth because he had been trained by skilled riders and had not been mishandled. "I agree," Lisa said again. "Unless he gets strong over fences, the snaffle should work well."

"Great," said Stevie. "We all agree. Then let's get out there."

Before mounting up, Lisa stopped for a moment in the driveway to touch the good-luck horseshoe. Carole and Stevie followed suit. Putting her left foot in the stirrup, Lisa suddenly felt self-conscious. "Hey, I never asked. Do you guys mind if I ride today?"

"Are you kidding?" Stevie said. "I'm so tired I'd probably fall off."

"Go ahead, Lisa," Carole added. "I'd rather watch from the ground today."

Lisa smiled with relief. The truth was, she felt a little sheepish. She had purposefully come to Pine Hollow early so that she could be the one to tack Samson up. And she'd been hoping that would naturally lead to her riding him. Her plan had worked, but it would have worked in any case. All she'd had to do was ask.

CAROLE STOOD IN the middle of the ring calling out instructions. "Remember, you're not riding Prancer," she advised. "Samson's going to need all the encouragement you can give him. Really sit down and settle him before each fence."

"Sure thing!" Lisa called happily from on top of the black horse. Her heart felt as light as a feather. She concentrated on making the approach to a small upright jump about two feet off the ground. Samson hopped over it in stride, almost as if it weren't there at all.

"Great!" Carole cried.

Lisa giggled. "After the brush, this must look like twigs to you," she whispered. It looked like twigs to Lisa, too! She was so confident on Samson, she felt she could jump anything. She felt almost incapable of making a mistake.

"Okay!" Stevie yelled. "I raised the top pole three inches!"

Carole called Lisa into the center. "Don't let the height bother you," she instructed. "It won't feel any different. Just think about the same basic points in your approach."

Lisa tried to keep a straight face. But she couldn't suppress a small laugh.

"What's so funny?" Stevie asked, joining them.

"It's just—on Samson, these little jumps feel like pick-up sticks," Lisa admitted.

"That's a great feeling," Carole said. "But no matter how talented a horse is, you don't want to rush him."

Lisa nodded gravely. She could hardly admit to Carole that after the brush she was . . . well, a little bored with the two-footers.

Carole watched Lisa trot off. She knew exactly how Lisa felt. When a rider got on a great horse, it was human instinct to want to test the limits. But a horse wasn't a car. Taken too fast, a green horse could sour, break down, go lame. The Macrae goal was going to be tough enough.

"How was that?" Lisa called.

"Good," Carole said. She could have given one or two pointers to Lisa, but she didn't want to be too bossy at this stage in the game. She knew Lisa would be sensitive to criticism. "I think by the end of this week we'll be able to take him around a little course."

Stevie stood up from the fence she was leaning against. "A course, huh? I hope I'm not on jump crew that day!" She wiped her face with the back of her hand. "I'm exhausted from fixing one jump!"

Though it was a hot Virginia morning, Lisa suddenly felt a chill run down her spine. In the elation of riding Samson, she had totally forgotten that she wouldn't be riding him every day. She reluctantly took her feet out of the stirrups, preparing to dismount.

"Want to walk him in the indoor ring?" Carole suggested.

Lisa nodded. "Sure." What she really wanted to do, at that very moment, was go cantering off to the woods, far, far away, where she wouldn't have to share Samson with anyone—not even her two best friends.

"I KNOW WE'RE all horse-crazy," Stevie announced one morning a couple of weeks later, "but this is the horse-*craziest!*"

Collapsed on trunks in the tack room, Lisa and Carole had to agree. Since Red had been away, they had lived and breathed horses from sunrise to sunset, sometimes staying till after dark to finish the day's tack. Lisa had arranged a schedule that incorporated Samson's training (in the early morning when Max was busy in his office), riding their own horses (in the afternoon), helping Max and Denise, who was Red's girlfriend and a part-time Pine Hollow employee, to exercise school horses and boarders (whenever they could fit it in), and doing a multitude of barn chores (morning, noon, and night).

They were all so busy during the day, and exhausted at the end of the day, that none of them had time to think. Lisa was glad. By throwing herself into the work at Pine Hollow, she had managed to forget about the Macrae— or at least her individual role in it. Instead she concentrated on the team effort: Project Secret Horse!

"You know, I fell asleep at dinner last night," said Carole, stifling a yawn.

"I fell asleep *before* dinner," Lisa responded. "My mom had to wake me up and drag me to the table."

Stevie grinned. "I ate my dinner in bed!"

Carole balled up a stable rag and threw it at her. "The important thing is, the plan is working."

"You'd better knock wood when you say that, Carole Hanson," Stevie insisted.

Carole rapped the table in front of them. "There. Anyway, I meant the plan is working *so far*. I don't think Max has a clue. Yesterday he asked me if we had found any time to ride Samson."

"What did you say?" Lisa asked, delighted.

"I told him he'd been out a couple of times."

The three of them giggled. In fact, Samson had been out every morning. The girls had taken turns riding him. Whoever wasn't riding served as jump crew, dragging the heavy standards and poles into place and raising or lowering them as needed. Carole had fallen into the role

59

of supervisor of the sessions. She was good at planning a productive hour, and Lisa and Stevie were happy to let her pace Samson's training. But they had contributed plenty of input as well.

Secrets aside, the training itself was going better than they had dared hope. It was going so well that the girls avoided discussing the subject in detail, afraid they would jinx it if they said anything positive. A superstitious feeling had seized all of them. They knocked wood and crossed and uncrossed their fingers.

"So what did you think of today's ride?" Stevie inquired. From her nonchalant tone of voice, she might have been asking what time it was.

Lisa gestured to Carole to go first. "Oh, I thought he did fine," Carole said in a bored voice. "You know—a few bugs to work out, but overall he was good. How 'bout you, Lisa?"

"Yeah, me too—same, I mean," Lisa answered listlessly.

But when the girls stood up to go saddle their next mounts, they were all grinning madly. The truth was, with Stevie aboard, Samson had jumped a difficult course flawlessly. It was the test they'd been waiting for. At the back of their minds the girls knew what they didn't dare say aloud: The Macrae was within their grasp.

A few minutes later, as they groomed two boarders on neighboring cross-ties, Carole brought up an idea she'd had. "I was thinking I ought to start riding Starlight in the mornings, too. That way we can school Samson and Starlight together," she suggested.

"Great idea," Stevie said. "When Samson gets further along, we could even have mini jump-offs."

"That would be fun. And we can also . . ."

Lisa stood frozen, dandy brush in hand, as her friends discussed the idea. All at once her hopes—and fears—had come flooding back to her. If Carole was still hoping to ride Starlight in the Macrae, then maybe she, Lisa, was going to get to ride Samson! This could be it! Her chance to vault into the big leagues. Lisa glanced sidelong at Carole and Stevie. Inside her a voice cried out, "Just tell them! Tell them you want to ride Samson in the show and see what they think! It's not like talking to Max. They're your best friends!" But before she could summon up the courage, Stevie had mentioned stepping up Part B of the Project.

"What's Part B?" Carole asked curiously. "I don't remember Lisa putting that in the schedule."

Stevie looked dramatically to her left and right. "Part B is the key to all successful surprise attacks," she said in a stage whisper. "Spying on the competition!"

* * *

WHEN CAROLE GOT home that evening, she was exhausted. But not so exhausted that she forgot to run out and check the mailbox. Carole always got the mail. It was one of her favorite chores—and the *only* one she never had to be reminded about. Unlike Lisa, who kept in touch with several pen pals, both overseas and in the United States, Carole hardly ever got personal letters. But there was always the chance that one of her horse magazines had come, or a program for a horse show, or a bulletin from Horse Wise, the Pine Hollow branch of the United States Pony Club. So Carole opened the box hopefully. Tonight's stack didn't look too promising, however. There was nothing big, which meant no magazines. Her expectations low, Carole sifted through a stack of bills for her dad, two identical entries for a publisher's sweepstakes, and a postcard reminding her that she was due for a dental checkup. She was about to shove the pile into her backpack when a letter fluttered out from between the two contest entries. It was addressed to her, and the return address was Old Stone Farm, Vermont. "Old Stone Farm!" Carole exclaimed. "That's Toby MacIntosh's place." She ran toward the house, holding the letter aloft. "Hey, Dad! I got a letter from Red!"

Carole wanted to savor the letter, so she waited till after dinner to read it. Then she stretched out on the couch and ripped it open. She laughed when she saw Red's handwriting. It was just like chicken scratching!

Dear Carole,
I got your letter a little while ago but haven't had two seconds to answer it. Toby works us pretty hard! That's great news about Samson. I only jumped him on the trail myself, but I could tell he loved it. I wouldn't be surprised if you had a good shot at the Macrae. I guess you intend to ride him? I'm sure the two of you could do well, but I know you'll be sorry to leave Starlight at home.

Startled, Carole sat up on the couch. She reread the last two sentences before going on to the end of the letter.

I wish I could be there to help you. If you have any training questions (since you can't ask Max!), feel free to call me at the number below. And don't worry, your secret is safe!
—Red

Frowning, Carole put the letter down. Her father was watching an old black-and-white movie on the VCR. Carole stared at the TV screen without seeing it. She had been so single-minded lately that the most obvious,

63

and important, question had completely slipped her mind. In all these days of zealous preparation, it had never once occurred to her: Who would ride Samson in the actual show?

Carole sat back against the couch, brooding. Subconsciously, maybe she *had* been planning to ride him herself. She had the most experience in showing, after all. And she had the connection to Cobalt, Samson's father. It seemed only right that she should be there when Cobalt's son made his jumping debut. But Red's letter pinpointed something else. Carole had also never considered *not* riding Starlight. From the moment she'd seen the Macrae program tacked to the bulletin board, she'd pictured herself and Starlight soaring over those gorgeous fences. Since *before* she'd seen the program, in fact. Since she'd first discovered *Starlight's* jumping ability. And if there was one thing Carole put a premium on, it was loyalty to her own horse. They had come this far together. No matter how much she cared for Samson, no matter how great a jumper the black gelding was going to be, she would never desert Starlight. It wouldn't be right.

"That settles that," Carole said aloud. Except that it didn't. The question still remained.

"What? You mean the ending?" Colonel Hanson piped up. "When's the last time you saw *Casablanca*?"

"What? Huh, Dad? Oh, I wasn't talking about the movie. I was just thinking aloud," Carole explained.

"Good," said Colonel Hanson, "because there are several major plot twists still to come. We're nowhere near a resolution."

Carole laughed. Watching old movies was one of her father's favorite pastimes. "When's the last time *you* saw *Casablanca?*" she asked.

Colonel Hanson thought for a moment. "Now that we own it, I like to pop it in every couple of weeks. So probably . . . two Thursdays ago."

Smiling, Carole said, "Then I'll have to watch it with you again in two Thursdays. Because right now I've got to hit the hay."

"Anything wrong?" her father inquired, muting the set.

Carole shook her head. "No, I've just got to think. There's a situation at Pine Hollow that Stevie, Lisa, and I . . ." Carole groped for a way to describe it so that her father would understand. "Let's just say we're nowhere near a resolution."

Colonel Hanson nodded. "You may be closer than you think," he said. "The easiest path is probably the straight one."

Carole raised her eyebrows. "Is that *Casablanca* talking?" she asked, surprised.

Colonel Hanson shook his head. "No, honey. You can learn a lot from *Casablanca* but not everything. That advice comes directly from one of the fortune cookies I ate at lunch."

"Oh, Dad!" Carole said. She tossed a pillow at him, which he deftly deflected.

As she stood up to go, Red's letter fluttered to the floor. Retrieving it, Carole noticed writing on the back that she hadn't seen before. She read it going up the stairs to her bedroom.

P.S. One thing I would recommend is exposing Samson to as many different courses as possible. The more kinds of jumps he sees, the better prepared he'll be for the Macrae.

An excellent point, Carole thought, brushing her teeth. As a green horse, Samson would be surprised by any new course he encountered. But his surprise might be softened if he had successfully negotiated a few strange courses before the Macrae. Making a mental note to talk to Stevie and Lisa about it in the morning, Carole climbed into bed.

She was nearly asleep when her brain clicked on something that brought her back to consciousness. She opened both eyes. But once she was awake she couldn't remember what it was that had occurred to her. "I hate that!" she murmured. Turning onto her other side, she tried to recall her train of thought. Exposing Samson to different jumps . . . Stevie and Lisa . . . making a mental note . . . Stevie . . . Lisa . . . *Lisa!* That was it! All week Carole had been noticing something about Lisa. But she had only just now *noticed* that she had noticed: Lisa had been acting strange lately. Carole couldn't put her finger on one single thing she'd said or done that was strange. But she still had the impression that something was bothering Lisa. Sometimes when The Saddle Club was talking, Lisa's face would fall. Or she would look as if she was about to say something, but then she wouldn't. It was almost as if she had a secret of her own—a secret besides their secret horse. Carole could think of any number of reasons why Lisa hadn't been herself. But before she could consider them, Carole was asleep.

FIRST THING THE next morning, Carole mentioned Red's letter. She omitted the question of who was going to ride Samson. That could be settled later. The important thing now was making sure Samson would need a rider at all. "The first thing Max is going to say when we ask him about the Macrae is, 'Samson's never jumped a single fence off Pine Hollow property.' But if he can get a few different courses under his belt—"

"Girth, you mean," Stevie corrected her.

Carole rolled her eyes. "Ahem, under his *girth*, then we'll already be one step ahead."

"Or one stride ahead."

"Or one *stride* ahead," Carole agreed, shaking her head at Stevie.

68

"Carole," Lisa suggested, "what about Mr. Grover's course?"

"That would be perfect," Carole said. "I'll bet he'd love to see how Samson's doing now."

"You've bet right," said Lisa. "Five minutes ago he was standing by Samson's stall admiring him."

"You mean—"

"Mr. Grover's here?" Stevie said.

Lisa nodded. She beckoned for the two girls to follow her outside. There she pointed to a two-horse trailer parked in the driveway. "I saw him come in. That's what made me think of it."

"But that's even more perfect!" Carole exclaimed. "Why don't we see if he can give us a ride over this morning?"

Lisa shrugged. "Sounds good to me. He's in the office talking to Max."

Stevie's eyes lit up. "I think it's time for me to go to work," she said. "You guys wrap Samson's legs for the trailer. Don't let anyone see you. I'll try to distract Max. When Mr. Grover comes out, nab him and let him in on the secret." She paused for a moment. "If anything goes wrong, say . . . say 'Hippopotamus,' " Stevie decided.

"Hippopotamus?" said Carole and Lisa in unison.

"Shouldn't we use a more normal word?" Lisa asked.

Stevie shook her head. "No way. If you choose a more normal word, somebody might use it by accident."

Giggling a little, the three girls split up. Carole went to get cotton and bandages from the tack room. Lisa went to put a halter on Samson. Stevie crept stealthily toward Max's office.

". . . other than the Macrae, not much to report," Max was saying. Stevie winced. A minute earlier and she would have heard the lowdown on the horse show! It wasn't fair.

"All right. I guess I'd better load up that horse and get going," said Mr. Grover. "It's been great talking to you, Max." There was a sound of chairs scraping back as the men stood up.

"Here, I'll walk you out," said Max.

Knowing she had no time to lose, Stevie burst into the room. "Hello, Max—Mr. Grover!" she said brightly.

"Hello, Stevie, how are you?" said Mr. Grover.

"Great," said Stevie, "but, um . . . Max, I've been meaning to ask you a question about last week's lesson. You see, lately when I ride Belle—"

"Excuse me, Stevie, but can your question wait a moment?" Max said. "I'd like to show Mr. Grover out."

"Oh. Okay. In that case, let's all go—out, I mean," Stevie said.

"Good," said Max. "In fact, I've got an idea. Why don't you help Mr. Grover wrap Gold Dust?"

70

"O-Okay," Stevie said uncertainly. "That's the new chestnut, right?"

"Right," said Max. "Last stall on the left. He's going over to Mr. Grover's for a couple of months."

Stevie thought fast. As she and the two men left Max's office, Carole appeared around the corner, carrying a pile of cotton and bandages. "Did you know that *hippopotamus* means 'river horse'?" Stevie said loudly.

Max gave her a sharp look, which Stevie ignored. Carole slowed in her tracks. "Oh, Carole—great. You can wrap Gold Dust with those. He's going over to Mr. Grover's today."

Carole raised her eyebrows but nodded. "Sure thing," she said, hurrying away.

"Now, Max, can you please answer my question?" Stevie said.

"Okay, what is it?" Max asked.

"I can't just say it. I have to demonstrate."

Max stared at Stevie suspiciously. "Stevie, I really—"

"Aw, go ahead, Max. Carole will help me with Gold Dust," said Mr. Grover affably.

"Very well," replied Max. "I'll give you about two minutes, Stevie, and then I really have to—"

"Max?" called a familiar voice. "Max?"

"Yes!" Max fairly shouted. "Oh. Sorry, Mom," he said sheepishly as Mrs. Reg came up to the group.

71

"There's a telephone call for you," announced Mrs. Reg. "Mrs. diAngelo on the line."

Stevie smiled with glee as Max's face got two degrees blacker. A call from Mrs. diAngelo was better than any time-wasting scheme of her own. With her silly questions and self-centered requests, Veronica's mother might keep Max on the phone all morning.

The second Max and Mrs. Reg had gone, Stevie hustled Mr. Grover down the aisle toward Samson's stall. "Mr. Grover, we need your help," she began urgently, then launched into an explanation of Project Secret Horse.

"Can you recap the training you've done so far?" Mr. Grover inquired when Stevie had finished outlining their plan.

"Sure. We started out really slowly with individual small jumps. Gradually we set up a course of jumps and raised the height to near where they'll be at the Macrae."

"Hmmm . . . And you think Samson's just as promising now as the day you discovered his ability?" asked the horse trainer.

"More so, if anything," Stevie replied. "He's still really green, but he knows what he's doing now. He's quieter; he goes at a steadier pace. And he's never refused a fence. Oops!" Stevie leaned over to the nearest stall door to knock wood. "Wouldn't want to tempt fate."

Mr. Grover was silent, thinking for a few moments. Finally Stevie could wait no longer. The Saddle Club was dying for a real professional's opinion. "So, what do you think?" she asked, crossing and uncrossing the fingers of her right hand.

"I think it's a fantastic idea!" Mr. Grover exclaimed. "I'd want to see the horse jump myself, of course—"

Stevie grinned. "That can be arranged," she said.

Briefly she outlined their idea for the day. "Count me in," said Mr. Grover. "Let's get him into the trailer before Max gets off the phone."

By that point the two had reached Samson's stall.

"We're ready and waiting!" Lisa called from inside. After a precautionary glance left and right, she and Carole led out the black horse, wrapped for travel.

"Was that part about Gold Dust a joke?" Carole whispered.

"No, I'm really taking him," said Mr. Grover. "But load up Samson first and then we'll go back for the chestnut."

The girls did as he said. Samson walked right onto the trailer, stuck his face into the hay net, and began munching. Only his black rump was visible from outside of the trailer. Meanwhile, Stevie had led out Gold Dust.

73

She was heading toward the trailer when Carole ran up to her.

"You forgot the bandages!" she whispered.

Stevie looked down at Gold Dust's legs. "Darn!"

"I'll get them," said Lisa.

Carole grabbed her arm. "Wait!"

The three of them froze as Max walked out into the driveway. "If he recognizes Samson, the jig is up!" Stevie muttered. Carole elbowed her to be quiet. Behind them a door was shut. Mr. Grover emerged from the truck. "All set? Oh, hi, Max. We're just getting loaded up."

"So I see. I didn't realize you had another horse in tow."

To keep from laughing nervously, Stevie focused intently on Gold Dust.

"Yeah, I'm taking this guy home. He's been at summer camp," said Mr. Grover, not missing a beat.

"Then, girls, hop to it!" Max ordered. "Get those bandages on Gold Dust so Mr. Grover can get out of here."

"Right!" Carole said, sprinting for the barn.

In a matter of minutes Gold Dust was ready to join Samson in the trailer. Max offered to help them load the horse. "Oh, no," Stevie said, "let us do it. You go on talking to Mr. Grover." Carole stood so that she blocked

74

Samson from view, Stevie put Gold Dust on board, and Lisa raised the ramp in a jiffy.

"You guys go with Mr. Grover!" Stevie urged. "I'll stay behind to distract Max."

"Deal!" Carole and Lisa whispered.

Stevie came out from behind the trailer. "Okay, Max. *Now* can I ask my question?"

Max threw up his hands good-naturedly. He said good-bye to Mr. Grover and followed Stevie toward the barn.

Ten minutes later, as the trailer rumbled slowly down the driveway, Carole let out a sigh of relief. "Phew! Now that we've stolen Samson, riding him should be a piece of cake!" she joked.

Lisa chewed her lip worriedly. "Yeah," she said quietly. "I guess you're right."

". . . SO WHEN I put my arm like this, my leg should slide back like that, but only if my head is turned in the opposite direction—"

"Stevie?" Max interrupted. "You've been explaining this new position for ten minutes. I still have absolutely no idea what you're talking about. Why don't you just stick to the riding positions outlined in the official manual of the United States Pony Club, okay? I think they should serve your purposes nicely."

"Okay," Stevie said, untwisting her arms and legs from the bizarre position they were in. By then she thought Mr. Grover and his cargo should be well out of sight. "I'll do that, Max."

Max let out a weary sigh. "Good. And now I've got to get back to work."

"Is there anything I can do to help you?" Stevie inquired, tagging along toward Max's office. "Lisa and Carole are gone on a trail ride, so I said I'd stay behind in case anything urgent came up here."

Max gave her a funny look. "That's very kind of you, Stevie. I appreciate all the work you've been doing, too. But I don't expect you to miss riding to help me, you know."

"But I wanted to, Max!" Stevie protested. "Honest!"

They had come to the door of Max's office. Max stepped through it. Stevie attempted to follow him, but Max barred the way. "Stevie," he said. He looked her in the eyes. "For heaven's sakes, go find something else to do!"

Stevie smiled wanly. "Okay, Max. If you're sure—"

"I'm sure!" The door shut abruptly in Stevie's face.

"Excellent," Stevie murmured to herself. "He'll be too scared to come out now."

With Max taken care of, at least temporarily, Stevie looked around for something to do. It didn't take her long. "Something" materialized in the form of some-

one—Veronica diAngelo, busy tacking up Danny on the cross-ties. Stevie eyed her prey from down the aisle. She was about to move forward for the pounce when she had a better idea. Quickly she got Belle out of her stall.

"Hello, beautiful," Stevie crooned. "Ready for some A.M. espionage? Nothing like a horse for camouflage," she muttered under her breath. Belle snorted in reply.

Putting a dejected expression on her face, Stevie led Belle out to the cross-ties closest to Danny. "Oh. Hi," she said glumly to Veronica, as if surprised to see her there.

"What, all alone today?" Veronica demanded. "I didn't know you could get out of bed without your two shadows to help you."

Stevie gave her a long-suffering look. "Carole and Lisa can't make it till later," she said, her voice gloomy. "Which is really too bad because we were supposed to go on a trail ride."

"Oh, were you?" Veronica said unsympathetically. "And now I suppose you want me to go with you."

Stevie raised her eyebrows. "Only if you want to. I mean—"

"Stevie Lake," Veronica declared, "your act won't fool me. You can save the innocent look, too—I know you want something. But I'll go on a trail ride if you like. Danny's had so many workouts with top-level trainers this week that he deserves a break. Don't you, boy?"

Veronica turned back to Stevie, hands on her hips. "So, we can do this together or not. What's it going to be?"

"Let's hit the trail," Stevie said, chuckling to herself. She didn't mind having her bluff called. She was sure all good spies were used to having to make a second attack.

On the trail Stevie got right down to business. She asked Veronica point-blank if anyone else was going in the Pine Hollow van with her to the Macrae.

Veronica smirked. "I knew that's what you were after. You still haven't abandoned hope, have you? Even though you and Belle wouldn't have a prayer of winning anything," she added.

"It's not for me, it's—!" Stevie began hotly. Then a lightbulb seemed to click on in her brain. If she let Veronica go on thinking that she, Stevie, was the one who wanted to go to the Macrae, she'd be able to get a lot more information out of her. Veronica wouldn't worry about being beaten by Stevie and Belle.

Belle was a wonderful horse. She could do dressage and jump, go English or Western; she'd been a Pony Club mount and a trail horse. But she wasn't an expensive Thoroughbred show horse. With a flash of understanding, Stevie realized how lucky this last fact was. "Oh, all right," she said, making her voice sound reluctant. "So I do have dreams about the Macrae. Is that a crime? You never know, Belle and I might do really well there!"

Veronica gave Stevie a patronizing smile. "Hey, there's nothing wrong with dreaming, Stevie."

Stevie had to turn her head away so as not to make puking noises in Veronica's face.

"As far as the van goes, I've rented out two of the stalls," Veronica said.

"Two?" said Stevie. "Are you bringing a second mount?"

"A second mount—aren't you silly? Why would I do that? Danny's all I need to win. Even Tom Riley agreed. He thinks—"

"Then why the second stall?" asked Stevie.

"For my stuff, of course!" said Veronica. "My tack trunk, my two saddles, Danny's special grain, my spare outfits, my—"

"Okay, okay! I get the picture," Stevie grumbled. Inside she was thinking, *But that still leaves two stalls open.* "So who has the other two stalls?" she asked as they picked up a trot.

"Search me," said Veronica. "Why should I care when I'm all taken care of?"

Stevie didn't trust herself to reply. For several strides she posted silently in the saddle.

Veronica was the one to speak next. Stevie felt the girl glance at her curiously. "Say, Stevie, if you want, maybe I could put in a good word for you with Max."

Stevie pretended to be thrilled. "Would you really?" she gushed. "It would mean *everything* to me. And Belle, of course."

"Sure," said Veronica, obviously relishing her role as benefactor, "I could do that. And you know, I'd be especially happy to try to help you if you could, you know, do a couple of little things to help me—like maybe give my boots a polish from time to time. Just as long as you understand that you'll probably come home empty-handed," she warned. "I wouldn't want you to get your hopes up and be disappointed."

Stevie gritted her teeth. To herself she said, *I won't be disappointed—not when I give my spot on the van to Carole and Starlight and they make you wish you'd rented out all four stalls for your stuff!*

Stevie was so focused on The Saddle Club's day of victory that she hardly heard it when Veronica invited her to come over to her house. "Huh? What did you say?" she asked absently.

"I said, it's silly for our Olympic-sized pool to go to waste with just little ol' me swimming in it. And I know you never have plans"—Veronica smirked—"other than hanging out *here*. So if you want to come over tomorrow, I could rearrange my schedule and plan to be home in the morning."

The condescending tone in Veronica's voice made Stevie want to strangle her. But every good spy had to sacrifice for the cause. Now was the crucial time to keep Part B of Project Secret Horse going full force. Clearly, Veronica adored the idea of Stevie as a pathetic hanger-on, desperate for a handout. And Stevie was more than happy to lay it on—thick as honey. "Really, Veronica?" she said, her voice meek. "Do you mean it? Swimming in the diAngelo pool would be the thrill of my entire summer!"

"I'll see you tomorrow then," Veronica said. "Mother will be so pleased. She does a lot of charity work herself, and she's always on my case to 'share the wealth.' "

Stevie nearly lost it then and there. Surely it couldn't have been this hard for James Bond. "Wow," she said in her most fawning voice, "I sure feel lucky."

8

"WHO'S GOING TO ride this bundle of energy?" Mr. Grover asked.

For a second Lisa thought he was talking about the Macrae. She stole a glance at Carole.

Carole was holding Samson's reins, and Samson, excited by the new setting, was dancing at the end of them. "I'll hop on," she volunteered. "Or you go first if you want, Lisa."

Lisa perked up visibly. "Really?"

"Sure. Let me give you a leg up."

Carole boosted Lisa into the saddle. Pleased as punch, Lisa walked Samson toward the ring where Mr. Grover's jumps were set up. Carole's eyes followed the pair speculatively. She had seen it again: that strange, un-Lisa-like expression. What did it mean?

Carole hadn't taken two steps when the most glaring truth hit her. "Of course!" she said aloud. It was so obvious, she couldn't believe she hadn't picked up on it sooner. Lisa wanted to ride Samson in the Macrae! It was the only explanation that made sense—the reason Lisa's mood seemed to rise and fall every time Samson and the Macrae were mentioned. But then why hadn't *she* mentioned it? Frowning, Carole leaned on the rail. The only conclusion she could come to was that Lisa hadn't wanted to step on anyone's toes. Lisa was very sensitive to other people's feelings. And she hated conflicts. If she thought either Stevie or Carole was hoping to ride Samson, too, she probably wouldn't mention her own desire to do so. Max would decide in the end, of course—if and when he agreed to Samson's going at all—but it was important that The Saddle Club present a united front.

Carole looked out to where Lisa had the horse moving at a brisk but collected trot. Samson's ears were pricked up, and he trotted along smartly. Lisa looked happy and confident. "They sure look like a winning pair," Carole said aloud, relaxing against the fence.

LISA FELT THE breeze on her face and the sun on her back. She sat straight in the saddle, heels down, elbows close to her sides. "This is the day I've been waiting for," she told Samson. "It's my chance to prove I can ride you in the Macrae."

Samson seemed to understand. The moment Lisa slid her outside heel back and sat down in the saddle, Samson picked up a rhythmic canter. A few minutes later, when Lisa asked for a trot again, Samson came back to her right away. More than satisfied with her warm-up, Lisa waved to Carole and Mr. Grover that she was ready to jump.

"We don't want to overdo it, Lisa!" Carole called. "So if I were you, I'd take him over those little jumps down at the end and then go ahead and jump the course."

Lisa nodded. "Sounds good!"

A few practice fences later, she was ready to try the set of eight fences. Carole came into the ring to give her some advice. "That one vertical is pretty big, so make sure you set him up right for it," she said.

Lisa almost had to feign seriousness. The jump that Carole was talking about was nowhere near as big as the Pine Hollow brush! *If she only knew* . . . , Lisa said to herself with a smile.

As was customary at the beginning of a jump course, Lisa trotted in a circle and picked up a canter. At Pine Hollow Samson had mellowed slightly, now that he had jumped the fences there several times. But today he was raring to go. He felt just the way he had the first day Lisa had jumped him. Lisa didn't mind; she was glad the horse's spirits were up. Her own were soaring!

The first few jumps went by in a blur. Dimly Lisa was aware that Samson was getting a little strong. She knew she ought to check him, but she almost hated to. Why not let him have his fun? What harm could come of it? None of these fences was big enough to bother a horse with his ability.

Midway through the course, the vertical that Carole had mentioned loomed ahead. A vertical was simply an upright fence with one layer of poles. Verticals could look less solid than other kinds of fences—less inviting, in horseperson's terms. Lisa saw Samson prick up his ears at the red-and-white poles. He weaved underneath her. Prancer did this sometimes, too, if a fence looked spooky. Lisa sat up in the saddle and urged the young horse on. Despite his curiosity, Lisa knew there was no question of his stopping in front of the fence. Samson didn't have a refusing bone in his body. In fact, he did just the opposite: He took off early—a stride too early. Completely unprepared for the huge jump, Lisa lost her balance. She expected to be tossed back into the saddle by the natural motion of the jump. Instead she was thrown farther forward. Dismayed, she felt her feet come out of the stirrups. She clutched desperately at the black mane. It was no use. With the impact of Samson's landing, Lisa was tossed into the air. She felt the dread of falling hit her. Then she hurtled toward the ground. She wanted to shriek—but it was too late. With a sickening crunch, the wind was knocked out of her.

At the rail Carole cried out. She charged toward her friend. "Don't move, Lisa! Don't try to get up!" she commanded. After a fall, a rider's instinct was to jump to her feet. But it was important to lie still, right where she had fallen, in case of broken bones or concussion.

For a few minutes Lisa concentrated on breathing slowly and answering yes-or-no questions about her condition. When she sat up, she saw Carole peering down at her. "Are you okay? Anything hurt? Can you talk?"

Lisa nodded as a feeling of shame overtook her. "I'm fine," she mumbled. The physical shock had been such that the mental shock was coming only now, a few minutes later.

Eventually Lisa was helped to her feet. "That was a real cruncher," Carole said sympathetically.

"I should have made him wait another stride!" Lisa said. "It was all my fault!" She stared numbly at the ground, reliving the last moments before the takeoff. "I let him get fast. I didn't even try to slow him down—"

"Oh, come on," Carole said, gently brushing the dirt from Lisa's shirt and breeches, "he's green! That was bound to happen. I'm just glad it happened now so that we can correct it. I mean—I'm not glad you had to fall, but just think, next time you'll know what to do."

"I guess," Lisa mumbled. Now that she knew she wasn't hurt, her disappointment was enormous. She could barely look Carole in the eye. Here she'd been out to prove how great she was, how she deserved to be the one to ride Samson in the Macrae! Hot tears came to her eyes, but she checked them. She wasn't going to let herself cry, not now in front of Mr. Grover.

Mr. Grover led Samson over. "He's a little shaken, but you'll calm him right down," the trainer said kindly to Lisa. "Are you ready to get back on?"

Panic seized Lisa at the idea of remounting. She had forgotten the necessity of getting back on a horse right after a fall. Otherwise, a rider could lose her nerve. Lisa nodded vigorously, hoping Carole and Mr. Grover wouldn't notice. "Sure," she said. "I'm just waiting for my leg up."

"You're sure, now?" said Mr. Grover. "I don't want to rush things."

"No, really—the sooner the better. Everyone takes a spill now and then, right?" Lisa said, making an effort to keep her voice light.

"That's a good attitude," said Mr. Grover. He held out his hands for Lisa to step into.

Once Lisa was on Samson's back, she realized the saying "The sooner the better" was true. If she'd waited any longer, she would have been too scared.

Carole went over to the vertical and dropped the top pole to the ground. That lowered the jump by six inches. "See how you feel, and when you're ready you can finish the course."

"Okay," Lisa said shakily.

Ten minutes later she still felt nervous. But she couldn't put it off any longer. Starting with the fence before the vertical, Lisa rode Samson around the course. This time she hardly even noticed the red-and-white fence. She hardly noticed anything. Her mind was set on finishing . . . finishing . . . finishing . . .

When it was all over, Lisa rode to the rail and dismounted in a hurry.

"You go ahead, Carole," she said. "I don't want to hog him."

"Okay," Carole said readily. "You did a great job getting back on, you know."

"Thanks," Lisa said wanly. "I'm going to go wait in the barn for a little while. I think the sun is getting to me."

At Carole's and Mr. Grover's concerned looks, Lisa tried to look more robust. "Be back soon!" she promised.

Inside the cool of the barn, Lisa leaned against a stall door. Her head was throbbing. What had gone wrong?

She had been riding along, completely confident, when all of a sudden she had hit the ground—hard. Sinking down onto a hay bale, she tried to tell herself it was no big deal. The truth was, every rider *did* fall now and then. If you didn't, you weren't a real rider. "But why did I have to fall today?" Lisa wondered aloud. Now she would never have the guts to ask if she could ride in the Macrae. It had been a wild dream, anyhow, she thought angrily. And it had ended the way wild dreams did: in disappointment.

Lisa didn't want Carole and Mr. Grover to worry, so after a few minutes she headed back out to the ring. She was just in time to see Carole finish what must have been a perfect course. Lisa could guess it was perfect based on Mr. Grover's burst of applause and Carole's ear-to-ear grin. Forcing herself to think of the team effort, Lisa strode forward, congratulations forming on her lips.

"You're our biggest ally yet," Carole said to Mr. Grover as he turned his pickup off the main road. The trainer was giving the three of them—two girls plus horse—a ride back to Pine Hollow.

"I'm honored to be included in the plan," Mr. Grover responded. "If you have trouble convincing Max, have him call me. I'll vouch for Samson's Macrae-readiness."

"We might take you up on that!" Carole said.

So that Max wouldn't suspect anything, the girls unloaded Samson at the top of the driveway. That way Mr. Grover could turn around right there and they could walk Samson the rest of the way to the barn. Both Carole and Lisa thanked their driver profusely.

"This was a great opportunity for Samson," Carole said again. "And for us."

Mr. Grover waved off the thanks and climbed back into the truck. "Say," he said curiously, "who's going to ride him in the show?"

Lisa turned her head aside, modestly allowing Carole to answer. The fall had erased all her hopes of receiving that honor.

"Max will have to make the final decision, of course," Carole said, "but it certainly won't be me."

Lisa caught her breath. Had she heard right?

"I'm committed to Starlight," Carole went on. "I think we have a good chance of doing well, and I couldn't let him down now."

"I'll second that," said Mr. Grover. He gave a wave and threw the truck into gear, leaving Carole, Lisa, and Samson standing there.

"So what do you say, Lisa?" Carole asked. "Are you up for it?"

Lisa stared. "But—But I fell off today!" she said, her voice trembling. "How could I ride him in the Macrae after that?"

Carole raised her eyebrows at her friend. "Since when does taking a spill have anything to do with getting back on and riding in a horse show?"

Lisa half smiled. "But I—I just assumed—"

"You assumed wrong. If you want to ride Samson, I'm all for it," Carole said as they headed down the driveway.

Lisa felt a rush of gratitude toward her friend. "Oh, Carole, I do! I do want to ride him—more than anything!"

"Great," said Carole as if what Lisa said was no big deal. "You might have to fight Stevie for it, but I doubt it. She's so busy competing with Veronica, I don't think she'll care about *actually* competing. So talk to her, and when the time comes, we'll try to convince Max."

Lisa felt dazed. After her days of worry, Carole had just handed her the opportunity on a silver platter. "You're not sad because of Cobalt—and—and everything?" Lisa asked.

Carole didn't say anything for a moment. Then she said quietly, "I thought about that. And you know, even if I rode Samson in the Macrae, it wouldn't bring his sire back."

Lisa nodded. Instinctively she understood that this was as important a moment for Carole as it was for her.

91

The girls walked a few paces in silence, Samson ambling along between them. When Carole finally spoke, it was in a totally different tone. "Besides," she said, "I've got Starlight to think of. And you know what? I miss him already!"

9

STEVIE WOKE TO sunlight streaming through her bedroom window. Another gorgeous summer day. She sat up happily. Without school and homework, she didn't even mind getting up early. She swung her legs over the side of the bed. Then she remembered where she had to go. All at once it seemed as if several dark clouds had covered the sun. She lay back down and pulled the covers over her head. Unfortunately, that didn't change the fact that she was due at Veronica diAngelo's in an hour.

"Why me?" Stevie groaned, putting on normal clothes instead of riding clothes for the first time that week.

With a scowl on her face, Stevie sat stonily through breakfast, barely hearing her brother Chad's comment about getting up on the wrong side of the bed.

"How would *you* feel if you had to go to the di-Angelos' for the day?" Stevie snapped.

"Veronica diAngelo's?" Chad said. "I thought you couldn't stand her."

"I can't!" Stevie wailed. "That's why I have to hang out with her today!"

Chad looked at Stevie's twin, Alex, his eyebrows raised. "Girls," Alex said succinctly.

Stevie gave them a withering glance. "This is a very complex situation involving high-level espionage," she retorted. But then her scowl grew deeper. "And I have to miss a day at the barn because of it!" she whined.

Chad shrugged. "Maybe it won't be as bad as you think."

"Yeah, you can hang out in that huge pool!" said Michael, Stevie's youngest brother. "They have a slide and two diving boards."

"And I'll bet they have good snacks," Alex pointed out. "With their private cook and everything."

Stevie sniffed. "That's true," she said. Maybe her brothers were right. Maybe the day would be tolerable if not pleasant. Even Veronica could have her bearable moments. Stevie was about to take another piece of toast when she stopped herself. "I think I'll save myself for the diAngelos'," she announced.

After helping her brothers clear the table and load the dishwasher, Stevie went upstairs and threw on an old bathing suit under her T-shirt and shorts. She took her bicycle out of the garage, hopped on, and headed over to the diAngelos'.

For most of the ride she was in good spirits. It was already hot out, which meant it was going to be sizzling by noon. So skipping a day at the barn wasn't the worst idea in the world. She even whistled a little in anticipation of diving into the cool, chlorinated water.

By the time she got close to Veronica's house, her anticipation was so strong that she forgot to look where she was going and ran over a sharp rock. She felt her back tire blow out. And there was nothing she could do about it. She didn't have a pump on her, and besides, she was almost there. There was just one hill between her and the Olympic-sized pool. She got off the bike and began pushing it. The hill had never seemed so long or so steep.

Finally the huge diAngelo mansion came into sight. Stevie wheeled the bike up to the house, leaned it against a large white column, and rang the bell. "Thank gosh that's over!" she said, trying to catch her breath.

A minute later a uniformed servant opened the door. "I'm sorry, we don't want any Girl Scout cookies," said the man in a disapproving voice.

Stevie jammed her foot in the door before he could close it. "I'm not selling cookies!" she panted. "I'm here to see Veronica. I'm a—a friend of hers."

The servant looked highly skeptical. "Wait here a moment," he said coldly. Leaving Stevie to sweat on the steps, the man disappeared again. After what seemed like forever, he returned. "Miss diAngelo says you may come in and wait in the library. She forgot you were expected and is in bed."

"She forgot?" Stevie said indignantly.

The servant ignored her. "She will be down presently. Please follow me."

Stevie followed the man down a hall and into a dark, book-lined room. As she took a seat in an armchair, he announced, "Please do not touch anything you can't afford to replace."

Stevie felt her blood start to boil. "Of all the rude—!"

"Yes, miss? Did you say something?"

"Who, me?" Stevie mumbled sheepishly.

The man fixed her with an evil eye before shutting the door behind him.

"Trapped!" Stevie said aloud, unbelievingly. "I'm trapped in the diAngelos' library!"

For twenty excruciating minutes, she sat sweating into the armchair. She didn't dare open a book for fear it would crumble into dust in her hands. She didn't dare leave the room for fear the butler—or footman or whatever he was—would catch her. "He'd probably lock me in the cellar and throw out the key!"

She tried to spy, but there didn't seem to be much to glean about the Macrae from the bookshelves and expensive-looking statues. Finally she couldn't stand it anymore. She rose and crept to the door. She was going to sneak out; it was now or never. Gingerly she placed a hand on the doorknob. To her surprise it twisted. Someone was opening it from the opposite side! Stevie sprang back as if she had touched hot coals. The door creaked open. Veronica stood there smiling.

"Why, Stevie. Hello! Jenkins told me you were here."

"Nice of you to get out of bed," Stevie muttered.

"Oh, really—it was no problem," said Veronica, completely missing the sarcasm. "Say, do you want something to eat?"

Stevie's eyes lit up. "And how! I bicycled over here and I'm dying of thirst and double-dying of hunger!"

Veronica led the way into the kitchen. Stevie noticed disapprovingly that her hair was elaborately curled and she was wearing a skirt and matching top. Stevie never wore anything nice for hanging out around the house. But then, she thought, maybe if your house was a mansion like Veronica's, every day was a formal affair!

"Let's see . . . ," Veronica said. Stevie watched hungrily as she rummaged through cupboards and then opened the refrigerator to stare inside.

Stevie's stomach growled. There was every kind of

cookie, cracker, and salty snack imaginable in the cupboards. The fridge was packed with juice drinks and soda. And standing on the counter was half a cake.

"Gosh, I don't know what I can give you," Veronica said, sounding disappointed. She turned to Stevie. "How about some water for starters?"

Stevie smiled wanly. "Water? What about a root beer?" she said.

Veronica looked stern. "Now, Stevie. You know as well as I that after exercising you should always drink water. Nothing else hydrates your body as well." She poured a glass and handed it to Stevie. "Now *I'm* going to have a diet orange, but my mother buys those specifically for me, because she knows I'm on a diet."

After gulping down the water in one long swallow, Stevie said pointedly, "Gosh, that cake looks terrific! What kind is it?"

"Where? Oh, that? It's devil's food." Veronica took the lid off the cake stand. She pinched a bite of frosting from one side and popped it into her mouth. Stevie stared at her the way a cat stares at a mouse. "I'd offer you some," said Stevie's host, licking her finger, "but it's a day old and that would be rude. Anyway, I'm on a diet for the Macrae. Hey, I know!" Veronica opened the refrigerator door again. "Carrot sticks! Mom always keeps plenty around."

Stevie felt faint. She clutched the counter. "Do you have any dip?" she murmured in desperation.

CAROLE WAS ENJOYING a leisurely breakfast. After the horse's big day the day before, she and Lisa had voted to give Samson some time off. That meant they could show up at Pine Hollow an hour or two later. Carole was glad of the extra time because she had something she wanted to discuss with her father: the issue of Lisa's riding Samson in the Macrae. Though she had been happy to cede the opportunity by not riding herself, Carole still wanted to make sure she was doing the right thing. Lisa had seemed very shaken after the fall. The fall itself wasn't such a big deal, but Lisa's reaction to it was. If she wanted to compete successfully in a show like the Macrae, she would have to ride with confidence.

With all his experience in the military, Colonel Hanson had a very good understanding of people—including Saddle Club members. And this was, Carole thought, a classic people question. Buttering an English muffin, she thought about how to phrase it.

The question of entering the Macrae, of course, was far from settled. Max might not agree to Samson's going at all. Veronica might not agree to their going with her in the van. And neither Carole nor Lisa had remembered to talk to Stevie to see how she felt about it. But

Carole had a hunch that all these things just might fall into place. "Dad?" she said tentatively.

Colonel Hanson looked up from the newspaper. "Yes, dear?"

"What would you do if there was a very important job to be done and—and someone wanted to do the job who was very enthusiastic but didn't have that much experience."

"Hmmm . . ." Colonel Hanson frowned in thought. "You mean if I were the person in charge and I had to choose?"

Carole pursed her lips. "No, not exactly. More like if you had to *recommend* someone to the, oh, the commanding officer."

Carole's father nodded. "So this person has no experience."

"Not *no* experience. She—they actually have a lot of experience. And they're good at what they do—very good, in fact. But this is a—an event that's more important than any event this person has participated in before."

"So let me see if I have this straight," Colonel Hanson said. "This upcoming event—you might say it was a kind of *debut* for the person, their chance to . . . to get a promotion, say."

Carole put down her English muffin. Sometimes her father amazed her with his insight. "That's exactly what it is, Dad," she said. "A promotion. At least," she added reflectively, "I'm sure the person sees it that way."

Colonel Hanson nodded again. He took a sip of coffee, sat back, and clasped his hands around one knee. "I'll tell you what I think, honey. In the Marines, there's no substitute for experience. That's why there are ranks: Even a very talented private can't do the job of a colonel."

"But, Dad—" Carole began to protest.

"But," her father continued, "I believe that every man—every man or woman, I mean—deserves a chance. So if the person isn't going to endanger himself or anyone else by being given that chance, then I would recommend that person for the job."

Carole spent a moment absorbing all this. "Oh, Dad!" she cried. "I knew you'd agree!"

"Agree?" said Colonel Hanson in surprise.

"Yes. *You* know," Carole supplied impatiently, "that Lisa deserves to ride in the Macrae!"

"AND THIS," SAID Veronica, flipping a page in her photo album, "is the family on vacation in Mexico when I was seven."

Stevie's eyes swam. Her head was pounding. On her lap Veronica held the second album she'd forced Stevie to admire. She had another six waiting in a stack on the couch.

101

"Now, here's our first trip to the Caribbean." Veronica took a long sip of her diet orange soda.

The Caribbean, Stevie thought longingly. Through the windows she could glimpse the blue water of the pool.

"Or was this our second? Hmmm . . . I can't remember. It must have been our first, because—"

"Speaking of the Caribbean," Stevie interrupted, "don't you want to go swimming? The water looks great."

Veronica gave Stevie a pained look. "Go swimming? Right after curling my hair? I don't think so. Now, let's get back to the album, because we have six more to—"

"Well, maybe I could go. And you could watch me," Stevie suggested.

"But that wouldn't be fun for me," Veronica complained.

Stevie glared at her. "Oh, in that case, forget it. Because *I'm* having a *won*derful time looking at photo albums!"

"I knew you would, Stevie!" Veronica exclaimed.

Hundreds—thousands—of photographs later, Veronica ran out of diAngelo family vacations. "Let's go up to my room," she suggested.

"Anything'll be better than this," Stevie mumbled, following Veronica up a wide marble staircase. Actually, she was slightly curious to see what Veronica's room looked like. Her mild curiosity deserted her, however, the minute she stepped over the threshold. In its place came white-hot jealousy. Of all the spoiled-brat rooms Stevie had laid eyes on, Veronica's was by far the spoiledest. She had everything—no, Stevie realized, she had *two* of everything! She had two beds, a huge television and a small one, two phones (one cordless), two enormous closets stuffed with clothes. She had a computer, a clock radio, a stereo—and they all looked new. She had a dressing table and chair, a wall of teddy bears, a shelf of horse models . . . The room went on and on and on—and opened up onto a little balcony overlooking the Olympic-sized pool. Glancing around, Stevie suddenly had an inspiration. "Wanna play horse models?" she asked, eyeing the large collection. Even Veronica couldn't ruin horse models, could she?

Veronica thought for a minute. "Okay. Why don't I be the beautiful show horse and you can be the ragged, broken-down nag, and I'll tell you stories about my glamorous life on the A circuit—"

"Or we could go swimming," Stevie interrupted flatly.

"Stevie," Veronica said icily, "I'm beginning to think you're here to use the pool, not for my company. That's not true, is it?"

"Of course not!" Stevie assured her with all the enthusiasm she could muster. "It's just that when Carole, Lisa, and I play horse models—"

Veronica stamped her foot on the plush white rug. " 'Carole and Lisa! Carole and Lisa!' Is that all you can talk about? Why don't you try getting some more sophisticated friends!"

That did it. The insult to Carole and Lisa was more than Agent Lake could put up with. Clenching her hands, she stared at Veronica. If she could control herself for another few minutes she might be able to escape without sabotaging the entire mission. "I have to go," Stevie announced. "I just remembered I have to—go."

"But I haven't even taken you on the grand tour!" Veronica complained. "And you haven't admired all my stuff!"

"I know!" Stevie groaned. "I know!"

Veronica's eyes narrowed. "You know, Stevie," she said menacingly, "I have plenty of other friends who would love a space in the van to the Macrae."

Stevie could endure it no longer. Throwing caution to the wind, she laughed aloud at Veronica's scare tactics. "It's not like you own the van!" she retorted. "It belongs to Pine Hollow, in case you've forgotten!"

Veronica's face turned white with anger. "So? I could get my mother to rent out the whole thing—all four stalls. She'd do it in a second, and then you'd be nowhere! You'd be high and dry!"

"You know what?" Stevie yelled. "I *am* high and dry!

Right now! And hot and sweaty! And you know what else? I did come over here just to swim! And I'm taking a dip in the pool before I leave!"

Ignoring the shocked expression on Veronica's face, Stevie looked around wildly for an escape. Her eyes lit on the balcony doors. Before Veronica could stop her, Stevie slipped through them and out onto the little terrace. "Now I'm trapped again!" she murmured. *Think, Stevie! Think! What would a spy do in a situation like this?* she wondered. *Something dramatic,* she decided. *Like slide down the*—"Drainpipe!" Stevie cried. She boosted herself onto the balcony wall. She seized the drainpipe with two hands and swung her legs over the edge.

"Don't you dare, Stevie Lake!" Veronica roared, racing out after her.

But it was too late. Eyes closed, Stevie pushed off and zipped to the ground. "Ow!" She sat down hard. But she was up in a flash.

"What are you doing?" Veronica screamed down at her. "You can't go in my pool without my permission!"

"Oh, can't I?" Stevie challenged. She ripped off her T-shirt and shorts and strode to the diving board. She took three gleeful running steps and cannonballed into the pool. She made a huge, satisfying splash. When she came up for air, she could hear Veronica's footsteps, first muffled, then clattering out onto the patio. Stevie swam over to the closest side. She pulled herself out of the water, a triumphant grin on her face.

Too late Veronica appeared, shaking her fist in anger. "Stevie Lake! I'm going to have my mother—I'm going to see to it that you—"

"Yes?" Stevie taunted her.

But Veronica had stopped midthreat. Her look of rage dissolved into one of utter amusement. She laughed hysterically. She pointed at Stevie and laughed as if she would never stop.

Alarmed, Stevie stole a glance behind her. There was no one there. With a sinking feeling she looked down at her bathing suit. Or rather, what had been her bathing suit. The ancient garment had finally given up the fight. It had ripped right up one side. With increasing horror Stevie saw that it had split into two separate pieces. And the two separate pieces were flapping in the breeze.

The urge to run screaming from the patio hit Stevie full force. But she resisted. Instead she raised her head and sniffed loudly. Nose in the air, she walked at a dignified pace to the little pile that was her clothes. She pulled them on over the tatters of her wet bathing suit. She shoved her feet into her sneakers. "I believe I'll be going now," she said in the snobbiest voice she could muster.

With Veronica snorting hysterically behind her,

Stevie pushed open the gate in the fence surrounding the diAngelos' pool area. She ran around to the front of the house and seized her bicycle. She got a running start up the driveway . . . and pedaled like mad, flat tire and all.

10

THAT AFTERNOON CAROLE and Lisa were saddling school horses when Stevie burst into the barn. "Hi, guys, sorry I'm late."

"You're not late," Carole said.

"Yeah, we thought you were going to be working on, ahem, Part B of the project all day," Lisa said.

"That was Plan A," Stevie explained.

"*Part* B was *Plan* A?" Carole inquired skeptically.

"Right."

"So what's Plan B?" Lisa asked.

"Show up at Pine Hollow and hang out with you guys."

"Uh-huh. And what happened with *Part* B?" asked Carole.

"Part B was a bust. I don't have what it takes to be a spy," Stevie admitted sadly. "After looking at nine million snapshots of the diAngelos' vacations, something in *me* snapped." Her voice grew grave. "I just couldn't take it anymore."

"Well, I hope you got valuable information before you left," Carole said sternly.

"Yeah, or at least told Veronica off!" Lisa added.

"I did tell her off," Stevie said. "But she got the last word anyway." Briefly Stevie related the bathing suit incident.

"Malfunctioning equipment?" cried Lisa in mock indignation. "Your headquarters should have taken care of that!"

"As far as information," Stevie said, "all I know now is that thanks to my failed mission, Veronica is doing everything in her power, as we speak, to prevent any of us from getting a foot—or rather, a hoof—anywhere near that van. She was talking about renting out the whole thing."

The three girls sighed in unison. "I did hear Mrs. Reg say Mrs. diAngelo was on the phone about a half hour ago," Lisa commented.

"That's nothing, though. She calls every day," Carole pointed out.

"True," said Lisa. "And look on the bright side,

Stevie. At least you got to look at all those fascinating pictures of—" Lisa's final words were lost as Stevie smothered her in hay.

When they had settled down, Carole persuaded Stevie to tack up a horse and take a trail ride with them. Stevie chose Barq, a pretty Arabian that Max had owned for years. When they were ready, the girls led the horses out into the driveway and got on.

"Boy, am I glad you two are with me today instead of Veronica," Stevie said. "Talk about a waste of a good trail ride. How was Mr. Grover's, anyway? I was so busy keeping Max at bay I barely got a chance to ask you yesterday."

"It went really well," Carole responded. "Mr. Grover thinks Samson's going to be ready for the Macrae."

In the midst of Stevie's enthusiastic replies, Lisa noticed that Carole had left out any mention of her fall. That was like Carole: She would never say anything to make any of her friends feel bad—or even any of her enemies. That, to Lisa, was true confidence. Lisa felt that way herself—about schoolwork. She never bragged about all the A's she took home, knowing how much harder it was for some of the other kids. Still, she thought she ought to mention what had happened. When there was a pause in the conversation, she spoke up. "I took a spill yesterday, Stevie," she said.

"How'd that happen?" Stevie asked.

Lisa explained about the jump, how Samson had left out a stride and she had reacted too late to stay on.

"That's great!" Stevie exclaimed.

"Great?" Lisa said uncertainly.

"Sure." Stevie turned around in the saddle to explain. "You know how it is with falls. Once you have one it's like having money in the bank. Now you won't fall again for a long time."

"Knock wood, Stevie!" Carole sternly instructed.

Stevie reached out to the next tree they passed and rapped a branch. "Seriously, though. It always happens that way. Now you're probably safe till next year. Or at least till well after the Macrae, which is the important thing." Turning back around in her saddle, Stevie thought of something else, something she'd been meaning to talk to Lisa and Carole about. "Say, you guys? With all this work we've been doing to train Samson, has it occurred to either of you that someone's going to have to *ride* him . . . in the Macrae? I mean, he can't jump those junior jumper courses himself. Well, he *could*, but I don't think the judges would be too happy about it."

Carole waited a moment before saying, "We were actually wondering how you felt about that."

"Me?" Stevie said. "Oh, no. This is between you two. I can't make the choice, it wouldn't be fair. Now, Carole, you did have a special attachment to Cobalt, a very

111

special attachment. And you have a lot of horse show experience. But Lisa, you discovered Samson's ability. You took the first risk by jumping him at all. And it would be a great opportunity for you . . ."

Lisa and Carole let Stevie go on weighing the alternatives for several minutes. Finally Lisa said, "But what about you, Stevie. Do you want to ride him?"

Stevie laughed heartily. "That's a good one. You think I, Stevie Lake, could be *paid* to put on a jacket and breeches in the middle of summer and compete against dozens of Veronica wannabes? Ha, ha, ha, ha, ha. Tell me another."

Now it was Lisa and Carole's turn to laugh. When they'd had a chuckle over Stevie's unqualified no, Lisa said, "But Stevie, you're normally so competitive."

"Yeah, I'm competitive," Stevie said. "But I'm not . . . *competitive*."

Stevie's friends didn't have to ask what the difference was. They knew exactly what she meant. Each of them was competitive in some way—but, thankfully, they were competitive in different ways.

Carole explained that between her and Lisa the matter was settled. "Then what are you doing dragging me into it?" Stevie complained.

Rounding a bend in the trail, the small group emerged from the woods into a meadow. Lisa had to blink hard in the sun. She felt as if she were blinking hard inside, too.

112

It was decided then, at least among her friends, at least among The Saddle Club: She was going to ride.

THE NEXT DAY The Saddle Club was back to early-morning schooling as usual. After the trail ride the girls had sat down to map out some particulars. They knew they couldn't put off revealing their hopes to Max much longer. The show was less than three weeks away. To prepare properly, they would need real instruction from him as soon as possible. Reluctantly Carole had suggested making the next day—today—the dress rehearsal. If it went well, they would stage the demonstration the following afternoon. If it didn't go well . . . "We'll cross that bridge when we come to it!" Stevie had declared.

As planned, Carole was riding Starlight and Lisa was riding Samson. That left Stevie, moaning and groaning, to be the solitary jump crew. "You realize I'm not doing this out of friendship!" she warned, dragging a pole over to a pair of standards.

"We know!" Lisa said. "You're doing it out of enemyship!"

"You're darn right. And if one of you doesn't beat Veronica, you owe me! Big!"

The combination the girls were schooling over was difficult. A combination was any set of two or more jumps placed close enough together so that each affected how the rider took the other. For instance, there might be a first fence followed by a tight turn to a second fence. Or a fence that had to be jumped at an angle so as not to miss the second fence. Carole knew that at the Macrae, the courses would be extremely technical and challenging. Anything was fair game.

"I can't seem to turn early enough after the first fence," Lisa said after two failed attempts. "Our angles are all wrong. I don't know if it's me or Samson."

"Do you want me to try him once or twice and see if I can get him through it?" Carole volunteered. "You could follow me on Starlight."

"That would be great," said Lisa. She was happy to have Carole school Samson over a rough spot, especially if she could learn from Starlight at the same time. Because now more than ever, every second counted.

The two of them dismounted and made an efficient switch of horses. Stevie was about to relinquish her position on the rail to see if they needed any help when she heard a noise behind her. Turning her head, she saw that the noise was the impatient, repetitive tap of a crop against a boot. A tall black boot. A well-worn tall black boot. A boot she recognized. *Max's boot!* Stevie looked up. Max was walking directly toward the ring.

Stevie glanced desperately toward Lisa and Carole. Both of them were intent on circling for the combination. It was too late to do anything, to warn them, to tell

114

them not to jump. Max was already standing beside her. "Have you seen Veronica?" he demanded.

Stevie shook her head. "She doesn't usually, uh, show up this early."

"I know that," Max said shortly. "But she signed up for an early-morning private lesson this morning and she's half an hour late."

"Oh," said Stevie. She was too nervous to say anything else.

"All right, I just wanted to check and make sure she wasn't out here. I'll be in the barn if anyone needs me." Max turned on his heel.

Stevie crossed her fingers. She held her breath. She prayed. She willed him to keep walking. And then he stopped. And spun around. "Is that Samson?" he demanded.

"Um . . . no?" Stevie tried.

Max came closer. "Yes, it is. It is Samson. I'd recognize him anywhere."

"Except in the back of a trailer," Stevie mumbled.

"What? What did you say?" Max looked closer. He frowned. "What are you doing with fences set up? He doesn't jump yet."

Stevie gulped. She stared straight ahead. Out in the ring, Carole cantered straight ahead. She cantered toward the combination and flew over the first fence. She made a tight turn and flew over the second fence.

115

Lisa, a few paces behind on Starlight, followed suit. Carole yelled something to Lisa. The wind carried her words over to the rail. "Let's finish the course!" she cried. Stevie saw Lisa nod and urge Starlight on. Stevie didn't move a muscle. Their dress rehearsal had just become opening night.

Carole led the way, crouched over the black horse's neck. They took two fences on the rail, turned down the diagonal, and flew over a fence in the middle of the ring. Samson jumped each jump with two feet to spare. Carole clearly had to struggle to keep her balance. But she did it. Finally they headed for the tires. Carole put the horse into it just right. She landed smoothly and pulled up just in time to see Lisa make a nice landing behind her. "Great job!" she called.

Pleased with her performance, Lisa pulled up, too. Side by side, the two of them jogged toward Stevie for a critique. But Stevie, they noticed, was not alone. She was sharing the rail with someone. In the same moment, Carole's and Lisa's brains made the click of recognition. The someone was Maximilian Regnery III.

LISA AND CAROLE wanted to turn tail and run. Or at least stand still and think up excuses. Instead they were drawn toward Max as if he were a magnet. They inched over to the rail, staring down at their hands.

"That *looks* like Samson," Max remarked dryly. "But as I was saying to Stevie, Samson doesn't jump yet."

There was an excruciatingly long silence. Carole and Lisa fiddled with their reins. Stevie picked at a loose wood chip on the rail.

"It's my fault, Max!" Lisa cried, unable to bear his disapproval any longer. "It's all my fault! I was riding Samson one day, and without thinking I—"

"But we went in on it with you!" Carole protested. "We're just as much to blame."

117

"I am, you mean!" Stevie corrected her grimly. "The plan was my idea!"

Max waited, his lips pursed in bewilderment, as the gathering descended into an angry fight over who deserved more of the blame for teaching Samson to jump. Eventually, though, the girls became aware that Max was watching them and saying nothing. They quieted down in embarrassment.

"So were you ever planning to tell me?" he inquired.

"Oh, yes! As soon as we were ready. Tomorrow, in fact," Carole explained anxiously. "We were going to give you a demonstration of Samson's jumping abilities tomorrow."

"Why tomorrow in particular?" Max asked. "Why not a month from now?"

"A month?" Lisa blurted out in surprise. "But that would be after the Macrae!"

Carole and Stevie froze, waiting to see how Max would take this second bit of news. Then Lisa realized what she had said. "You see . . . that's what we're training him for," she added, fumbling along, seeing no way out of a real explanation. "We—We want to enter Samson in the junior jumper division of the Macrae Valley Open."

Max ran a hand through his hair. He gave a long, low whistle. "Junior jumpers at the Macrae," he said. "That's a tall order."

Neither Lisa nor Carole nor Stevie dared move. A part of each of them had hoped—secretly hoped—that Max would love the idea the minute he heard it. That he would give them an instant stamp of approval. That he would cry, "I wish I'd thought of that myself!" But Max was a horseman. He was responsible for his horses and his students. By necessity he was very careful about giving his approval for anything, let alone a daring scheme like The Saddle Club's.

Max put a hand to his forehead to shield his eyes from the sun. He looked at each one of them in turn. "I'll tell you what. My morning lesson doesn't seem to be showing up. Cool off, untack, and come to my office so we can talk."

The Saddle Club nodded solemnly. They watched Max start toward the barn. They were so wound up by that point that they almost missed it when he turned around to say, "By the way: Nice ride, you two."

When he was safely gone, Stevie and Carole started talking at once. Stevie was sorry she hadn't thought fast enough to distract him. Carole said at least he'd caught them in a good moment. "And saying, 'Come to my office,' is hardly a flat-out no," Carole pointed out. They both began to plan for the meeting in his office.

"We should say he at least has to let us give him the demonstration we planned!" Stevie said.

"With anyone else I would agree. But it's Max," Carole reminded her. "He's seen enough to judge."

"Hmmm . . ." Stevie twisted her mouth around, plotting madly. "Maybe I should run up there now and start mucking stalls," she suggested. "So all our barn work will be fresh in his mind."

Carole laughed. "He'd know exactly what you were up to."

"I guess," Stevie admitted reluctantly. "But maybe if I just brought a pitchfork to the meeting—"

While her two friends grew more and more animated, Lisa remained silent. She had never felt less like a team player. She couldn't seem to pay attention to what Stevie and Carole were saying. From the moment she had recognized Max at the rail, one creeping fear had preoccupied her: Max had seen Carole taking Samson around the course—perfectly. How would she ever convince him that she could do as well?

TWENTY MINUTES LATER The Saddle Club shuffled into Max's office and took seats on folding chairs. Max came out from behind his massive desk and perched on the corner. "You guys have a spokesman to plead your case?" he asked.

There was an uncertain pause. Then Carole and Stevie cast sideways glances at Lisa. She could talk to adults better than anyone.

120

Lisa, feeling their eyes on her, stood up tentatively. She started to speak, slowly at first because she was very nervous. But she built momentum as she went. It wasn't a hard argument to make, after all, for she believed every word she was saying. "I think Samson pled his own case out in the ring this morning, Max," she began. "As you saw, he's a phenomenally talented jumper. And we've been working hard to train him. Carole has set up all kinds of courses here at Pine Hollow, and two days ago we went to Mr. Grover's to practice over his jumps. Mr. Grover, by the way, supports our efforts. He said you could call him to discuss Project Se—er, to discuss the project. We know the Macrae is a major show, and we know it's ambitious to want Samson to make his debut there. But"—Lisa faltered before continuing passionately—"but a top racehorse doesn't start on a backyard track! Samson deserves a shot at the best—*now*—early on in what promises to be a brilliant career. And Carole, Stevie, and I believe that when the Pine Hollow van pulls out of the driveway for Pennsylvania, Samson by Cobalt out of Delilah deserves to be on it!"

Awed by Lisa's skill in argument, her two friends broke into applause. Lisa sat down, her face flushed. Even Max couldn't hide how impressed he was. "That was quite a speech," he said. As The Saddle Club watched, he paced back and forth across the office floor. His heels clicked rhythmically against the wood. "And

121

you're right about one thing: Samson did plead his own case in the ring, half an hour ago." The Saddle Club sat forward on their chairs. Max paused to stare reflectively out the window. "He reminded me of Cobalt," he said, his voice suddenly hoarse. When he spoke again, he sounded as if he was talking to himself.

"There would be logistics to be worked out, of course. The diAngelos have already rented out two stalls of the van, and they'd like all four."

"All four! But that's ridiculous!" Stevie cried. "You can't take a van hundreds of miles to the Macrae with one horse in it! It's—It's wasted space!"

The faintest of smiles played on Max's lips. "I happen to agree. If we're going to make the trip, I'd like to bring a whole team from Pine Hollow." He turned to Carole. "I had thought you might want to ride Starlight. But if you're set on bringing Samson, I'll agree to that as well. With your experience, you two might have a real shot at it."

As Max began to outline the work that needed to be done in the next few weeks—if, indeed, they were going—The Saddle Club sat frozen. Carole stared at their instructor and shook her head from side to side, willing Max to understand. After what seemed like an eternity, Max paused, frowned, and demanded, "Why the long faces? Didn't you hear me? I've just agreed to let you go ahead with your idea. I've agreed to Samson's going to the Macrae."

"The thing is, Max," Carole said quietly, "I do want to ride Starlight. It's been my dream for years to take him to the Macrae."

"But then—"

Lisa tensed in her chair. It was now or never, and she had to speak for herself. She couldn't wait for the others to plead *her* case. She thought of soaring over the brush fence on Samson's back. Summoning all her courage, she said boldly, "And I want to ride Samson."

Max's eyebrows went up and then down. He looked surprised. "I see," he said seriously. He stood up from the desk. "I would have to think about that," he said in a tone that betrayed nothing. He took another turn around the small room. "Of course, I would also have to see you ride, Lisa."

Lisa gulped. That was only fair. "When?" she said, her voice barely audible.

"Anything wrong with tomorrow?" Max inquired.

Lisa shook her head. "No. Tomorrow's fine," she got out.

"All right, then," said Max, all business. "Tomorrow it is."

From his tone The Saddle Club knew that they were dismissed. In one motion they stood up. As they did,

Stevie's pitchfork clattered to the floor. "Whoops," she said sheepishly.

Max picked it up and handed it to her. "The stalls on the far aisle are ready and waiting," he informed them.

FOR ONCE NOT complaining, Stevie grabbed a wheelbarrow and led the way to the far aisle. She knew Lisa was anxious, and she knew Carole was anxious about Lisa. To diffuse the tension, Stevie acted like a drill sergeant. She handed out tools and told the other two to get to work. Then she turned on the barn radio to an oldies station. "Nothing cures the blues like hard work and fifties music," she declared. "Come on, Lisa, hop to it. That stall has your name on it."

Bent over her pitchfork, Lisa was glad to be distracted by physical labor. She felt as if it were the day before a big exam. She couldn't allow herself to think about Max's decision. If he said no to her riding Samson, the disappointment would be so great . . . She shook her head vigorously to clear her mind. She concentrated on the words to the fifties song. She concentrated on doing the best job mucking a stall ever. The decision was out of her hands.

THAT NIGHT, LISA sat listlessly at the dinner table. As usual, her mother prattled on about her day while her

124

father listened. Lisa picked at her spaghetti and tuned in and out of the conversation. "Oh! I saw Mrs. diAngelo at the post office," her mother said. "I think she knows me by now, but I reintroduced myself to make sure. I reminded her that our daughters ride together at Pine Hollow and that we were on that horse show committee together. You're right, Lisa, Veronica is going to the Macrae Valley Open. Evidently she's expecting to do very well. They've hired several professional trainers— top trainers—to get her ready. And I guess—"

"They always do that, Mom," Lisa interrupted grumpily. "It doesn't necessarily mean she's going to win."

"Really?" said Mrs. Atwood. "Mrs. diAngelo sounded pretty confident."

"Tons of people could beat Veronica," Lisa insisted. "Carole could beat her!"

"Is Carole riding in the show?" asked Mrs. Atwood.

Lisa nodded. "Almost definitely."

Lisa's mother was silent for a moment. "But if Carole's riding, then why can't you—"

"I can't talk about it, Mom!" Lisa cried. She stood up from the table, her face red.

"Lisa," said her father gently, "sit down and finish your dinner. Your mother's only looking out for you."

"That's right, honey. Sit back down," added her mother, patting Lisa's chair.

Lisa swallowed hard. She sat back down. "I'm sorry, Mom. I'm just nervous, I guess. I have a—a test at the barn tomorrow."

Mrs. Atwood nodded understandingly. "As long as you've studied, you'll be fine," she said. "Now, who wants dessert?"

IN HER ROOM, Lisa sat on the bed, her knees drawn up to her chest. " 'As long as you've studied, you'll be fine,' " she repeated to herself. Her mother was right. And she had studied—or in this case, practiced. She had practiced hard, and she was ready. But then another thought occurred to her. Maybe she should *study* study—study for real! She had crammed for tests at school before. Why couldn't she cram for a riding test? It couldn't hurt, could it?

She sprang off the bed and went to her bookshelf. She took down every book she had on riding, except the dressage books. She opened the first one and turned to the section on jumping. Marking the text with her finger, she feverishly began to read. *"Jumping a horse is not a science. It is an art. The most important lesson for the rider to learn . . ."*

126

12

SOMETHING ABOUT THE light was wrong. Lisa went on sleeping, but she knew the light was wrong. She turned over . . . yawned . . . She sat bolt upright, utterly panicked. She didn't even have to look at her clock to know the awful truth. She had overslept by an hour!

"How could I?" she wailed. In one motion she was out of bed and across the room. Fighting back tears of frustration, she dug out a pair of breeches and pulled a T-shirt over her head. "Mom! I'm late! I've got to go!"

In the car riding to Pine Hollow, Lisa was beset with fears. She had spent half the night studying books on jumping. In consequence she'd gotten little sleep. She was exhausted, physically and mentally. And instead of helping her, the riding books had only made her more nervous. They talked about things she didn't even know she was supposed to be doing—like "creating the perfect arc" over a fence. Plus, the whole experience had reminded her of a jumping problem she'd had a long time before, with Prancer. Lisa had gotten over that problem (it had been mostly nerves, anyway), and if she had learned anything, it was that confidence was everything.

Hurrying into the barn, she remembered something else. She had skipped breakfast. She felt weak, worried, and tired. She didn't even know if she had the energy to put Samson's saddle on. She almost wanted to give up then and there—convince Carole to ride in her place or Stevie to change her mind. Then she saw her two friends. They were leading Samson out to the driveway. He was fully tacked up. "Oh, good—you're here," Carole said. "We were going to warm him up for you."

"You were?" said Lisa, astonished.

"Yeah, we figured you were taking an extra hour or so to psych up at home," Stevie responded.

"Hardly! I was actually taking an extra hour to sleep through the alarm!" Lisa said bitterly. "Is—Is everything okay? Is Max waiting?"

Carole noticed the panicked look on Lisa's face. "Everything's fine, Lisa. Max got delayed by another call—this time from Mr. diAngelo. He'll be out in ten minutes. But listen, are you okay?"

"I'm fine! I'm just great. I can't wait—" Lisa broke off midsentence. She looked at Stevie and Carole, her lower

128

lip quivering. "I'm actually really nervous," she said. "I—I don't know if I can do it."

Carole opened her mouth to commiserate when Stevie interrupted. "Nonsense!" she said. "You've already done it—for us, dozens of times. This is just a formality for Max. It'll be a breeze! Now put 'er there. I'm giving you a leg up."

Before Lisa could protest, Stevie had boosted her onto Samson's back. Laughing, Carole handed up a hard hat, which Lisa buckled on. They all walked down to the ring together. Warming up, Lisa decided to take Stevie's attitude. "Maybe it will be a breeze," she said aloud. It was as good an attitude as any.

ALL THE NIGHT before, Lisa had been worried about what Max would have her do: what kind of course he would set up, how high he would make the jumps. So she was completely taken aback when Max appeared, leaned against the rail, and said simply, "All right, show me what you can do, Lisa." After a quick consultation with Stevie and Carole, Lisa determined to do just that.

Carole set up a cross rail, which Lisa and Samson trotted back and forth over. Stevie added a vertical beyond it. Lisa smiled with joy when she felt Samson's huge jump. He *gave* her confidence even when she didn't have much to begin with. Cantering over the course Carole had ridden the day before, Lisa relaxed fully. She concentrated not on showing herself off, but on showing Samson off to the best of her ability. The difficult combination loomed ahead. Lisa checked Samson several strides before it. She saw his ears go up. Then he shied beneath her. "What are you looking at?" Lisa said aloud. She barely had time to steady him before she saw what had spooked him: a soda can glinting in the sun at the base of the first fence. Someone must have dropped it there and not picked it up! But who would be so rude? So careless? There was no time to answer that question. They were coming into the fence—and they were coming in all wrong! Lisa made a split-second decision. She sat down hard. She pulled back on the reins. And knowing she might be ruining her chances at the Macrae, she wheeled Samson around—away from the fence.

Trying desperately not to get upset, she made a circle and reapproached. This time Samson hit it just right. The second fence followed easily. But Lisa could feel herself losing hope. She had to finish the course! She had to go on! There were two fences left. The first was the white chicken coop. Samson cleared it easily. Then only the tires remained.

At the rail, Stevie and Carole crossed their fingers. Carole saw the mistake first. "Oh no," she murmured. "Her approach is all wrong!"

"Shhh!" Stevie hushed her. "Max'll hear!"

Twenty feet away Max was also watching intently. His lips were pursed skeptically. Lisa was way off course.

Carole covered her eyes. She couldn't bear to watch. How could Lisa mess up something so easy as the last fence?

Stevie felt her blood run cold. "She's going to take the brush," she said.

Carole's eyes snapped open. "What?"

The two of them gripped the rail in front of them. It was unbelievable. Lisa was headed straight for the brush.

"Come on, Samson!" Lisa cried. And the big horse responded. *Finally,* he seemed to say, *a fence that's big enough for me!* Lisa grabbed his mane wildly. She clung on for dear life. And then . . . it was over. They were on the other side. There was nothing to do but slow up. And for a split second, Lisa didn't care one bit whether she got to ride in the Macrae Valley Open. Fences like that made it all worth it, no matter what happened. Her eyes shining, she turned for home. Stevie and Carole were climbing down from the rail and running toward her.

"That was amazing! That was incredible!"

"*You* were incredible!"

In the midst of their ecstatic congratulations, Lisa noticed a lone figure walking back up to the barn. But she wouldn't let herself worry—not now, not yet. She had

131

done what Max had said: She had shown what she could do. She could only hope it would be enough.

THE DAY PASSED in a blur of barn work. It was so hot Stevie hosed herself down from time to time. That, of course, meant that she hosed down anyone else who happened to go by. But Carole and Lisa were glad to get cool. Drying off on the knoll, they specifically avoided discussing Max's pending decision. Carole and Stevie knew it would only make Lisa nervous. But when they were back mucking stalls, Stevie slipped away and ran down to the outdoor ring. Making sure she wasn't being followed, she slid through the fence and darted over to one of the jumps. She leaned down and grabbed the soda can. Sure enough, it was a diet orange. Stevie's eyes narrowed into two slits. She had a funny feeling that her spying was about to pay off.

Meanwhile, Carole quietly went to Max's office. She knocked firmly on the door. "Come in!" said Max, looking up wearily from a stack of papers.

Carole cleared her throat. She wasn't as great a speech maker as Lisa, but she had something to say. Without waiting for Max's encouragement, she launched in.

". . . and so, I believe that every woman—or man— deserves a chance," she concluded a few minutes later. "And the Macrae Valley Open is Lisa's."

Max pushed his chair away from his desk. He formed a stack of papers and tapped them into order. "Have you three ever considered debating?" he asked. "If not, you ought to. The other teams wouldn't stand a chance."

Carole didn't know whether Max's joking was a good sign or a bad sign. She waited, hearing the tick of the clock on the wall.

Finally Max smiled. "I think Lisa deserves a chance, too," he said.

"Yes!" Carole cried.

"I had to think about it because the horse is so green and the competition is so tough. But if she knows she can do it, then she *can* do it."

"Max, that's great!" Carole exclaimed. "It will make Lisa's day! It'll make her year!"

"I'm counting on you and Starlight to train with them," Max said sternly. "And to help them out at the show."

Before Carole could reply, there was a hesitant rap on the door and Lisa walked in. Seeing Carole, she stood still awkwardly. "I'm sorry. I didn't mean to interrupt, but I—Well, the truth is, I know you said you'd decide based on this morning, Max, but I think I deserve a chance to tell you why I deserve to ride!"

Max put up a hand. "I just got that speech," he said, "from Carole. The answer is yes."

133

Lisa was dumbfounded. "It is?" she said.

Max nodded. "What do you think all this paperwork is? It's two sets of entries for the Macrae!"

Lisa and Carole shrieked and hugged each other. As they embraced, there was a third knock. Stevie came in carrying a pitchfork and an empty soda can. An empty diet orange soda can.

Max took the can from her without asking what it was.

"Don't you want me to explain exhibit A?" Stevie asked.

"I think I have a pretty good idea where—and whom—it came from," Max said tersely. "I think someone is going to spend some time doing ground cleanup. I'm sure it wasn't dropped on purpose, but I wouldn't want to discover any more trash lying around where someone could get hurt."

The Saddle Club remained silent, but Stevie couldn't help letting a small smile flit across her face. Still, she knew from experience that when Max took things into his own hands, it was better to stay out of it—way out of it.

"And you can stop carrying that around, too," Max commanded. "I know how much barn work you've been doing, and I appreciate it, okay?"

"But I like carrying the pitchfork around!" Stevie protested. "It means I'm always ready to muck a stall!"

Amid the girls' celebratory chatter, Max stood up and waved his hands for silence. "I do have some bad news," he said, looking at Stevie with concern. "As you know, I only have two free stalls in the van. If Carole and Lisa both ride, I won't be able to take you, too, Stevie."

"I don't care about not riding," Stevie said readily, "if that's what you mean. I intend to go as a stable manager."

Everyone stared at this pronouncement.

"Stable manager?" said Lisa. "But you hate barn chores!"

"In general, yes," Stevie admitted. "But I'm not above getting my hands dirty to help the, *ahem*, common cause."

Max looked perplexed. Unfortunately, The Saddle Club had to let him stay that way. They couldn't explain that the common cause meant one thing: beating Veronica!

WHEN STEVIE AND CAROLE cleared out, Max held Lisa back a moment. "Lisa," he said seriously, "you had quite a ride this morning, jumping the brush instead of the tires at the end. That's one big fence."

Lisa blushed with pride. "I wanted to convince you I could do it—that Samson and I can jump any obstacle we meet."

Max nodded. "That's great. But I want you to understand something. My decision had more to do with the way you handled the combination than with the spectacular jump you threw in at the end."

Lisa frowned. "Really? But I had to approach the combination twice. In a show, that would have counted as a refusal."

"Yes," Max said, "it would have. But in a show, as at

home, safety comes first. You thought fast and remained calm this morning. You made the right decision out there. And I'm proud of you. That's why I'm letting you ride."

Lisa nodded. She felt a world of understanding open up to her. "Thanks, Max," she said. "You won't regret it."

DINNER AT THE Atwoods' that night was a different story. Lisa was so excited she could hardly sit still. She waited until the meal had been served before sharing the good news with her parents. Mrs. Atwood set the plate she was holding on the table. "My little girl is going to compete in the Macrae Valley Open?" she said incredulously.

Bursting with joy, Lisa nodded. "Max just okayed it this morning."

"I—I can't believe it!" Mrs. Atwood cried. She hugged Lisa. "I'm so proud of you! All your hard work has paid off!"

"Congratulations, honey," said Lisa's dad. "I don't know exactly what the Macrae is, but it sounds like a big honor."

"Big honor?" Mrs. Atwood scoffed. "It's the biggest! I can't wait to tell my friends in the P.T.A.! We'll have to get you a whole new outfit. Oh, gosh, I hope I run into Mrs. diAngelo soon!"

Lisa shifted uncomfortably. Now that she had made her announcement, she wished her mother would drop the subject. But Mrs. Atwood talked nonstop through dinner.

"Imagine if you won the trophy! Dad and I would get to go to the winners' circle. I wonder if there's a party afterward? What's the date? I'd better make a haircut appointment. I'll have to look my best in the spectator stands. This is so exciting. To think: the Macrae Valley Open Horse Show. One of the biggest society events of the year!"

By the time dinner was over, Lisa was exhausted. She crept up to bed, leaving her mother talking on the phone with one of her friends. "Do you realize what an honor this is? My Lisa! . . ."

Despite her fatigue, Lisa didn't sleep well. She should have been happy. Her dream had come true, after all. But every several months, maybe twice a year, Lisa had a recurring nightmare. The plot was always the same: She would dream that she was going into a major exam. On her way into the classroom she would remember that she had forgotten to study, that she knew absolutely nothing about the subject. The teacher would hand out the tests. "But I forgot to study!" Lisa would plead. "Can't you give me a break?" "I'm sorry," the teacher would say, "but you know I can't help you." Lisa would look down

138

at the test paper, certain she was going to fail. Then she would wake up.

She had the dream that night. She woke up at dawn in a cold sweat. "Thank goodness it was only a dream," she said aloud, relieved as she always was. But this time the feeling of relief didn't stay with her. She tossed and turned until the alarm went off.

After breakfast she read a book until her mother called and said she was leaving. "I'll drop you off at Pine Hollow, dear! I know you don't want to miss a minute."

Stevie and Carole were in the midst of haying and watering when Lisa arrived. "You can help Mrs. Reg with the grain," Carole advised.

Lisa conferred briefly with Max's mother, who handed her a list of horses to feed. "You go up the far aisle and I'll go down the near and we'll meet somewhere in the middle," said Mrs. Reg.

Lisa was glad when she saw that the last horse on her list was Samson. After dumping premeasured amounts of pellets and sweet feed into his bucket, she hung over the gelding's stall door. "I still haven't told anyone about the first time we jumped the brush," Lisa murmured. "It's our secret, boy. But did you hear? I'm going to ride you in the Macrae! Carole, Max—everyone thinks we can do it." Samson went on eating his grain with gusto.

Lisa wished he could talk. She wished he could reassure her that *he* wanted her to ride him. "I just hope I'm good enough to—"

"It's nice to watch a horse eat, isn't it?" said a voice behind her. Startled, Lisa spun around to see Mrs. Reg, empty grain buckets slung over her arm. "I always stop and look in myself when I'm done feeding."

Lisa nodded awkwardly, wondering how much Mrs. Reg had heard. "I guess you heard about me and Samson," she volunteered finally, wondering what Mrs. Reg would say.

"Yes, that's terrific news," said Mrs. Reg.

For some reason Lisa had expected her to say more. "So—So you're not surprised?" she asked.

"Why should I be surprised?" Mrs. Reg countered. "He's a lovely horse, and you're a good rider."

Lisa barely heard the compliment. "It's just—I don't have that much experience with training green horses, I mean, at least not compared to—"

"Pshaw!" Mrs. Reg interrupted. "What do you think Prancer was when you started riding her? She was fresh off the track. That's *worse* than green, harder to deal with, anyway. And you've done wonderfully with her."

"I guess so," said Lisa. Then, realizing how rude she must sound, she added, "I mean—thanks. Thanks, Mrs. Reg."

"You're welcome," Mrs. Reg said pleasantly.

"You know," Lisa added, her voice tentative, "I took a fall the other day—on Samson."

"Did you?" said Mrs. Reg.

"Yeah. Over at the Grovers'. We got into a fence wrong and I—well, I just fell off."

"You weren't hurt, were you?" asked Mrs. Reg.

Lisa shook her head. "Oh, no! I was fine, Samson was fine, and I got right back on and jumped the fence that gave us problems."

"Good," said Mrs. Reg. "You did the right thing."

You did the right thing. That was what Max had said the day before. Lisa knew that this knowledge ought to have comforted her, but somehow it didn't. "I—I guess I did," she said worriedly.

Mrs. Reg gave her a searching look. "Is something bothering you, Lisa?" she asked.

Lisa felt her face redden. "Oh, no! Everything's great," she said. "I'm riding in the Macrae! What more could I want?"

"Well, I'd better go up to the house," Mrs. Reg said finally. "Deborah is going to D.C. all day, so I'm baby-sitting."

"Say hi to little Maxi for me," Lisa said, relieved that Mrs. Reg wasn't launching into one of her famously long-winded, enigmatic stories.

"I will," Mrs. Reg promised. Reflectively she added,

"It seems like yesterday Maxi was a newborn, doesn't it? And now she can crawl like lightning, pull herself up . . . She'll be walking in no time. But babies—kids—are amazing that way. They're all confidence. They can do anything they put their minds to. It would never occur to a baby to think, Maybe I'd better not try to walk; there's a chance I could fall down. They just fall a hundred times and keep right on going."

"Sure, Mrs. Reg," Lisa said vaguely. "I, ah, had better get going, too. We're cleaning all the bridles before lunch today."

Soaping reins in the tack room, the girls discussed the competition at the Macrae. "My mother's all excited because the Macrae is a big society event in Pennsylvania," Lisa remarked.

Carole nodded. "It sure is. This show is really for the richest of the rich. These girls all have the most expensive saddles, the most expensive boots—heck, I bet they go to the drugstore and ask for the most expensive hair nets!"

Stevie snorted with laughter. "I wonder if their horses eat special grass!" she joked.

"If it exists, you bet they do," Carole said.

Lisa rinsed her sponge in the bucket on the floor. "Carole, I know you're kidding and all," she said, "but you don't think we'll be outclassed, do you?"

142

"On Samson and Starlight?" said Carole. "Hardly. And anyway, we can't worry about that. At every show you go to, there's somebody with a fancier horse or a fancier trainer—or a fancier everything. You just have to have faith in yourself and your horse. That's what counts."

"I'm sure some of the other girls are at least . . . nice, right?" said Lisa.

"I wouldn't count on it," said Carole. "Look, I'm sure a few are, but I haven't met any—except Kate, of course. In fact, I once had a girl cut in front of me in the line for the toilet, even though she knew I was on deck to ride!"

Lisa put a hand to her mouth in horror. "You're kidding!"

"Nope."

"What did you do?" Stevie asked.

Carole laughed, remembering. "What could I do? I rode the course . . . in *pain!*"

"Speaking of pains," Stevie said, "I think a certain someone finally showed up—for *yesterday's* lesson."

"Max must have been furious!" Carole said.

"He was. But she begged him to squeeze her in, so they're out there now. Say," Stevie suggested, "wanna go check out the competition?"

"And how!" Carole said.

"Lisa?"

143

"Sure," Lisa said, though a part of her would rather have stayed behind.

Using the excuse of bringing in horses from the pasture, The Saddle Club trooped outside. They each clipped a lead shank on a horse and, as casually as possible, edged toward the outside ring. The grass there was much thicker than in the pasture, where it had been grazed over for weeks. The horses were happy to put their heads down to eat while Stevie, Lisa, and Carole watched the goings-on in the ring.

What they saw was less than uplifting. In fact, it was pretty darn depressing. Whether it was her trainers, her determination, or, Stevie thought, her carrot-stick-and-diet-orange diet, Veronica looked really, really good. She barely seemed to move in the saddle as Danny cleared a huge course of six jumps.

"He might just live up to his name after all," Carole remarked.

The truth was, Danny was a great horse. And Veronica was a good rider. When she made the effort, she could ride very well. Evidently the Macrae was a big enough show for her to make the effort.

"Let's not watch anymore. I'm feeling sick," Stevie announced.

Carole laughed. "Too sick for a lunch break?"

"No way!" Stevie said.

Absently Lisa was aware of her friends calling to her

to come inside with them. But she stood, looking not at Veronica but at an object in the ring. She couldn't tear her eyes away from the brush jump. It was gigantic. It was a towering, frightening obstacle. Had she and Samson really jumped it? Twice? It seemed impossible. Lisa couldn't pinpoint when it had happened, but a terrible feeling of doubt had seized her. Now it wouldn't seem to let her go.

The calling grew louder. Stevie and Carole weren't just calling her name. They were calling another name as well. Lisa closed her eyes, turned away from the brush jump, and reopened them.

"Red!" she heard. "Red's back! Lisa, come say hi!"

Lisa clucked to the horse she was leading. "Come on, girl, we've got to go say hi to Red!"

14

"LISA, HI! Carole told me the great news!" Red exclaimed as Lisa joined the group assembled by Red's pickup truck.

"Thanks, Red," said Lisa. "How was your time at Toby MacIntosh's?"

"Great!" he said enthusiastically.

Immediately Carole began to batter him with questions about the horses he'd ridden, the lessons he'd taken, what he'd learned—

"Let the man breathe!" Stevie interrupted.

Red grinned. "It's okay. I'm happy to answer as many questions as you want about Old Stone Farm—"

"Including what Toby eats for breakfast?" Stevie joked.

"Health food cereal!" Red shot back. "And black coffee."

"Eeeuuw!"

"I'm happy to answer any questions," Red continued, "but first I've gotta get something to eat! I've been driving for two days and the motel I slept in had lousy food. You girls want to come with me?"

The Saddle Club cheered their response. "We'll be right back!" Stevie promised. The three of them turned and led their horses into the barn. After depositing them in the right stalls, they met up in the aisle.

"It's great that Red's back, isn't it?" Carole said. "It's like the whole barn breathes a sigh of relief."

"It's like *I* breathe a sigh of relief!" Stevie said.

"And how!" Lisa agreed. When Stevie and Carole ran for the pickup, Lisa dashed after them happily.

No sooner had they squeezed into the cab of the pickup than Max appeared, leaning against the driver's side door. "Hi, boss," said Red.

"Welcome home," Max said warmly. "We sure are glad to see you."

"Max!" Stevie wailed. "Didn't we do a good job?"

"The best," Max said. "But it's still nice to have my right-hand man back."

Red explained that they were all going to grab lunch and would be back shortly.

"How about if I come, too?" Max said. "I'll follow in my car."

"Sure. Sounds good."

Max stood back to let them go. "And I'll treat, too—to welcome you back, Red, and to thank you girls for all the hard work you put in while Red was gone. What do you say to . . . TD's?"

Stevie, Lisa, and Carole were delirious with happiness. "*Max? Treating us to TD's?*" Stevie shrieked. "Ice cream for lunch? I think I'm in heaven!"

At Tastee Delite, the three girls claimed their usual booth. Red took an adjoining table for him and Max. When Max arrived, they saw he had brought Mrs. Reg. And Mrs. Reg had brought Maxi.

"It's turning into a party," Stevie said gleefully.

After the waitress took their orders, the adult table fell to talking about Pine Hollow business.

The kids' table chattered away about nothing at all—the weather, ice cream flavors, horse stories. Lisa found herself laughing and talking easily with her friends. The strange, fearful mood that had held her in its grip seemed to be fading away. When their sundaes came she did something she'd been meaning to do for a long time: She thanked Stevie and Carole for their support.

"No matter how I do, riding in the Macrae is the most incredible chance for me," Lisa said, and she meant it.

148

"Maybe you'll win and I'll get second," Carole tossed out, just because it was fun to imagine.

"Vice versa would be fine with me," Lisa said, grinning.

"Just concentrate on doing your duty," Stevie joked, "not to Samson or Starlight or Max or your parents but to me, Stevie Lake, a girl with a mission. Remember, Project Secret Horse is still secret from Veronica."

Max turned his head toward them. "Did you ask about Veronica? She couldn't come. I invited her but she had lunch plans already."

"Oh, too bad," said Stevie with a wicked grin. "What's she doing, dining at a four-star restaurant?"

"I don't think so," said Max. "She told me she had to hurry home because Tom Riley is coming over to discuss strategy with her."

"Tom Riley?" Red said. "I met him up at Old Stone Farm."

"You did?" Carole said.

"Yeah," Red replied. "Toby had him up one weekend to teach a guest clinic on show jumping."

"He's supposed to be very good," Mrs. Reg said, bouncing her granddaughter gently on her lap. "I always see his face on the cover of riding magazines."

"Like *Sporting Horseman?*" Lisa asked impishly, kicking Stevie under the table.

"No, I don't know that one, but lots of others," Mrs. Reg said.

"I hear he's excellent as well," Max said. "What did you think, Red?"

"Oh, he's a great teacher, no doubt about that. He taught *me* a lot anyhow. He's also a nice guy. He's got a lot to say about making a living in horses. It's tough, I guess."

The Saddle Club stared at Red. Stevie dropped her spoon into her dish.

"It's tough?" she repeated.

"Absolutely. Tom has to coach all kinds of students because it pays well. He said he gets some real spoiled brats. He said—"

But Red couldn't finish his sentence. The Saddle Club had erupted in laughter so loud that the waitress and the man behind the counter were giving them strange looks. Max, Red, and Mrs. Reg were used to the girls' outbursts, though. When the guffawing showed no signs of tapering off, Mrs. Reg kindly suggested to Stevie, Lisa, and Carole that they get their sundaes to go and take themselves out into the parking lot.

Outside, the girls finally managed to control themselves. "Do you think I have ESP?" Stevie asked.

"Maybe just Veronica ESP," Lisa said. "What do you think she's doing now?"

"Hmmm . . ." Stevie put a hand to her forehead. "I

150

picture her seated at a long table munching carrot sticks. There's a man there, a very successful rider, and he's . . . bored to death!"

Carole and Lisa laughed again. At this point they probably would have laughed at anything Stevie said. It was such a relief to know they were going to the Macrae, to know their project had worked. For once Carole didn't feel as if she should be knocking wood. Samson's training was no superstition: It was real. And Carole had high hopes for Starlight *and* Samson. She knew Lisa could do the job as long as she believed in herself.

The two girls leaned companionably against Red's pickup, watching Stevie's antics. Stevie had found a grassy stretch beside the parking lot and was turning cartwheels along it.

"Come on!" she yelled. "Doesn't anyone want to join me?"

"On a full stomach?" Carole said. "No thanks!"

Eventually, though, Stevie talked them into it. Lisa and Carole walked over to the grassy border. Stevie went, then Carole went, leaving Lisa standing alone on the parking lot side. "I always get scared about doing cartwheels when I haven't done them for a while!" she cried.

"C'mon!" Stevie yelled. "You can do it!"

Carole and Stevie jumped up in the air, imitating cheerleaders. "Go, Lisa! Go, Lisa!" they yelled.

151

Lisa grinned. With friends like The Saddle Club, she could do anything she set her mind to. All it took was confidence. With their cheering urging her on, she took a breath, raised her right hand, and turned three perfect cartwheels.

ABOUT THE AUTHOR

Bonnie Bryant is the author of nearly a hundred books about horses, including The Saddle Club series, Saddle Club Super Editions, and the Pony Tails series. She has also written novels and movie novelizations under her married name, B. B. Hiller.

Ms. Bryant began writing The Saddle Club in 1986. Although she had done some riding before that, she intensified her studies then and found herself learning right along with her characters Stevie, Carole, and Lisa. She claims that they are all much better riders than she is.

Ms. Bryant was born and raised in New York City. She still lives there, in Greenwich Village, with her two sons.

Don't miss the next exciting
Saddle Club adventure . . .

SHOW JUMPER
Saddle Club #87

The Saddle Club is going to a prestigious horse show!
Unfortunately, so is Veronica diAngelo, and she's al-
ready deciding where to display her next blue ribbon.
But Veronica may be in for a shock. The Saddle Club
has a secret weapon: Samson, the natural-born jumper.
He and Lisa Atwood could steal the show.

As Lisa competes, she realizes that Samson is even
better than they thought—and a lot better than she is.
And the other riders are mean-spirited and seem to
think winning means destroying the competition, not
just trying your hardest. Do Lisa and Samson have the
right stuff to take the blue? Or will they have to settle
for less than the best?